Blood in a Bordello

✪ ✪ ✪

From the room at the head of the stairs there issued muffled sounds that left little doubt as to what was going on behind the closed doors.

Slater tried to open the door, but it was locked. He knocked on it.

"We're busy in here," a gruff voice called.

Slater knocked again, then recognized the unmistakable sound of a pistol being cocked. He jumped to one side just as the shot was fired. A hole appeared in the door as the heavy .44 caliber slug tore through the wood.

Slater heard glass crash and a woman scream. He kicked the door open and rushed inside. A naked woman was standing by the bed, her skin nicked by glass from the window. Slater ran over to look outside. Then he heard a grunt of triumph from behind him and he turned quickly to see that he had been suckered.

Lattimore came at Slater with a knife. . . .

Also by Dale Colter

The Regulator
Diablo At Daybreak

Published by
HARPERPAPERBACKS

DALE COLTER

THE REGULATOR

DEADLY JUSTICE

HarperPaperbacks
A Division of HarperCollins*Publishers*

This is a work of fiction. The characters, incidents, and dialogues are products of the author's imagination and are not to be construed as real. Any resemblance to actual events or persons, living or dead, is entirely coincidental.

HarperPaperbacks A *Division of* HarperCollins*Publishers*
10 East 53rd Street, New York, N.Y. 10022

Cover art by Miro

First printing: May 1991

Printed in the United States of America

HarperPaperbacks and colophon are trademarks of HarperCollins*Publishers*

10 9 8 7 6 5 4 3 2 1

SOMEWHERE IN THE PRE-DAWN DARKness a calf bawled anxiously and its mother answered. In the distance, a coyote sent up its long, lonesome wail, while out in the pond, frogs thrummed their night song. The moon was a thin sliver of silver, but the night was alive with stars . . . from the very bright, shining lights, to those stars which weren't visible as individual bodies but whose glow added to the luminous powder dusting the distant sky.

Around the milling shapes of shadows that made up the small herd rode three cowboys. One was much younger than the others.

Known as "nighthawks," their job was to keep watch over the herd during the night, then turn them over to the drovers in the morning for the short drive into the railhead at Devil Pass.

"What do you mean? Are you trying to tell me you've *never* even had a woman?" one of the older cowboys asked the young one.

The cowboy, whose name was Billy, cleared his throat in embarrassment. "I'm only sixteen. I guess I never gave it that much thought."

"Why, boy, don't you know you can never be a man until you go upstairs at Big Kate's place?"

"With Big Kate," the other added.

"With . . . with Big Kate?" Billy asked in a plaintive voice that was decidedly void of any enthusiasm over the prospect.

"Hell yes, with Big Kate. Big Kate owns the place. That means ever'body who comes in there has to go with her first."

"Tell you what," the first cowboy said. "Why don't we ride into Devil Pass first thing after we get off work? It'll be daytime, there won't hardly be nobody else there, an' we can have our pick."

"All except Billy," the second cowboy insisted. "He has to go upstairs with Big Kate."

"Well, yeah, but then he can go upstairs with anyone he wants to."

"'Cept whoever me an' you have already took for our ownselves."

The calf's call for his mother came again, this time with more insistence. The mother's answer had a degree of anxiousness to it.

"Sounds like one of 'em's wandered off," Billy said. "I'll go find it."

"Hell, why bother? It'll find its own way back."

"I don't mind," Billy said, slapping his legs against the side of his horse and riding off, disappearing in the darkness.

One of the cowboys laughed, a low, knowing laugh. "If you ask me, Billy's just anxious to get away from us before we talk him into actually going upstairs with Kate."

"Who knows?" the other teased. "Maybe we can convince him she's just what he needs."

"I'd hate to see the fella that really needs her." Both cowboys laughed at their joke.

A loud, blood-curdling scream, filled with such terror that both cowboys shivered all the way down to their boots suddenly came from the darkness.

"What the hell was that?"

Billy's horse came running by, it's saddle empty.

"That was Billy!"

Though both were wearing guns, neither man was actually a gunman. Nevertheless, their friend was in trouble, and feeling the unfamiliar weight of pistols in their hand, they rode to his aid.

A moment later, gunshots erupted in the night, the muzzle-flashes lighting up the herd.

"Jesus! What's happening? Who is it? They're all around us!" one of the cowboys shouted in terror, firing his gun wildly in the dark.

The two men tried to fight back but they were young, inexperienced, scared, and outnumbered. In less than a minute, both had been shot from their saddles and then the night grew still, save for the restless shuffle of the herd of cattle.

At some distance away from all this, a short but powerfully built man sat on his horse with his hat pulled low over a bald head and browless eyes. Though he had put everything in motion, he had not, personally, taken part in the proceedings. Now one of his men, with the smell of death still in his nostrils, rode up to him.

"That's it, Pardeen," the rider said. "We kilt all three of them cowboys and took a look all around the herd. There ain't no one else ridin' nighthawk."

"Good. Now, take the cows," Pardeen ordered in a hoarse whisper.

Much later in the afternoon of that same day, about forty miles south of Devil Pass, Sam Slater stopped to give his horse a rest, and to take a drink of water. He took a deep drink, wiped the back of his hand across his mouth, recorked the canteen and hooked it over the pommel, then clucked at his horse to start him moving again.

It had been a long, hard ride, and Slater was butt-sore and saddle-weary. His was a bone-aching tired that went much deeper than mere trail weariness. It was a tiredness brought on by months of living on the edge, of eyeing every stranger suspiciously, of entering each town with his muscles tense, ready, if need be, for a lightning-fast draw and a deadly accurate shot.

Ahead of him, the little town of Sulphur Springs rose from the hot, sun-baked earth like a series of low lumps of clay and rock. Sulphur Springs was a one-street town that had grown up at this location to take advantage of the only water in the area, even though, as the name attested, that water was of questionable quality.

Sam was a tall man with ice-blue eyes and a scar that ran like a purple flash of lightning from his left sideburn down to the corner of this thin-lipped mouth. He squared his hat on his dirty-blond hair and urged his horse on into the little town.

Sam had reason to believe Jason Lattimore was in Sulphur Springs. Six weeks ago Lattimore had murdered a rancher and his wife, then raped the rancher's eighteen-year-old daughter, leaving her a soul-scarred shell of the vibrant, young girl she had been. After that, he killed the sheriff and the deputy who came to arrest him and boasted that he would never be taken alive. He left a note on the body of one of the men he had slain, saying that whoever came after him had better be ready to give up their own life.

Already a wanted robber and murderer, Lattimore's crimes against one of the leading families of the territory, and then against the sheriff and deputy who came for him, had so incensed the decent folk that they doubled the reward being offered for his arrest. Dead or alive, Lattimore was now worth $500.

Sam trailed Lattimore to Sulphur Springs because going after people like Jason Lattimore was what Sam did for a living. Sam was a bounty hunter, a man who specialized in hunting down the most hardened and despicable cases. Most of the men Sam went after were wanted dead or alive, and most, like Lattimore, had boasted that they would never be taken alive. More often than not, Sam accommodated them in that wish. As a result of Sam's efficiency in the deadly pursuit of his profession, he was known everywhere as "The Regulator."

Sam surveyed the town as he rode in. He had seen hundreds of towns like this. There was almost an ethereal quality to them, though of course, that was not a word in Sam's vocabulary. To him, Sulphur Springs was like all the other towns, a street faced by false-fronted shanties, a few sod buildings, and even a handful of tents, straggling along for nearly a quarter of a mile. Then, just as abruptly as the town started, it quit, and the desert began again.

In the winter and spring, the single street would be a muddy mire, worked by the horses' hooves, and mixed with their droppings so that it became a stinking, sucking pool of ooze. In the summer, it was baked hard as a rock. It was summer now, early afternoon, and the sun was yellow and hot.

The saloon wasn't hard to find. It was the

biggest and grandest building in the entire town. Sam knew that Lattimore would be there, and when he saw the horse matching the description he had for Lattimore's mount, he pulled up and dismounted. Walking over to the animal, Sam patted it on the flanks, then lifted its right rear foot to look at the shoe. There was a nick in that shoe that had been leaving a distinctive mark and Sam checked to make certain this was the animal he had been trailing.

It was.

Loosening his pistol in the holster, the bounty hunter walked inside.

Because of the shadows, there was an illusion of coolness inside the saloon, but it was only an illusion. The twenty or so customers who were drinking had to keep their bandannas handy to wipe the sweat from their faces.

Anytime Sam entered a strange saloon he was on the alert. He surveyed the place with such calmness that the average person would think it no more than a glance of idle curiosity. In reality, it was a very thorough appraisal of the room. He checked out who was armed, what type of weapon they were carrying, and if they were wearing their guns in the way that showed they knew how to use them.

Sam also checked to see if there was anyone he knew, or, more specifically, if there was anyone who knew him. It was particularly important for him to pick out such people, for there were many more people who knew him than he knew, and many of them could be gunning for him for one reason or another.

None of the drinkers seemed to pose a problem. From all he could tell, there were only cowboys and drifters here. Less than half were wearing guns. A couple of the cowboys were wearing their guns low and kicked-out, gun-fighter style, but Sam could tell at a glance that it was all for show. He was certain they had never used them for anything but target practice, and probably were not very successful at that.

The bartender stood at the end of the bar, wiping the used glasses with his stained apron, then setting them among the unused glasses. When he saw Sam step up to the bar, he moved toward him.

"Whiskey," Sam said.

The bartender saw the purple scar on Sam's cheek, and the pupils of his eyes grew larger. He poured Sam's drink with shaking hands, and Sam knew he had been recognized. He tended to have this effect on people, and he knew that even mothers sometimes frightened their children by saying, "If you don't behave, The Regulator will get you."

"Do you know who I'm looking for?" Sam asked quietly. His voice was low and rumbling, like distant thunder.

"I think m . . . m . . . maybe I do," the bartender stammered.

"His horse is out front," Sam said. He took a drink and eyed the bartender coolly. "But I don't see him."

The bartender raised his head and looked toward the stairs at the back of the room. "You're just not looking in the right place," he said.

"Thanks," Sam rumbled. He finished the drink then looked toward the flight of wooden stairs leading upstairs to an enclosed loft.

Sam pulled his gun as he started up the stairs. The others in the saloon, seeing Sam going up the stairs with a gun in his hand, stopped in mid-conversation to watch.

From the room at the head of the stairs there issued muffled sounds that left little doubt as to what was going on behind the closed doors. Normally, such sounds would elicit ribald comments from the patrons below. Today, however, there was no teasing at all. Everyone was more interested in the life-and-death confrontation that was about to take place.

Sam tried to open the door, but it was locked. He knocked on it.

"We're busy in here," a gruff voice called.

Sam knocked again, then, because he was tense and alert to the slightest thing, he recognized the unmistakable sound of a pistol being cocked. He jumped to one side just as the shot was fired. A hole, the size of a man's thumb and the height of a man's chest, appeared in the door as the heavy .44 caliber slug tore through the wood. Had Sam not moved exactly when he did, he would have caught that bullet in the heart.

Almost immediately after the shot, Sam heard glass crash and a woman scream. He kicked the door open with a splintering smash of wood and rushed inside. A naked woman was standing beside the bed, her skin nicked and cut by glass from the window. The floor was covered by long shards of glass and Sam ran over to look outside, expecting to see Lattimore down in the street.

Sam heard a grunt of triumph from behind him and turned quickly, to see that he had been suckered. Lattimore had broken out the window, then stepped back into the corner to fool Sam into thinking he had jumped out. Now, Lattimore was coming at Sam with a knife in his hand and he made a long, stomach-opening swipe. Sam barely managed to avoid the point. One inch closer and he would have been disemboweled.

"Drop the knife!" Sam shouted, bringing his pistol around to bear on Lattimore.

"Get out of here!" the naked woman suddenly screamed, unexpectedly hitting Sam on the gunhand with the chamberpot.

"What the hell?" Sam shouted in surprise as he saw his gun clatter to the floor.

"Good woman!" Lattimore barked and he came toward Sam again, lunging at him with his knife.

Sam dropped to one knee so that the knife-blade passed overhead. He felt around on the floor trying to grab his gun but it was just out of reach. Instead, his hand wrapped around a long, dagger-shaped shard of glass. Without a second thought, he picked it up, and using it as a knife, thrust it deep into Lattimore's abdomen. Hot blood spilled across his hand. Lattimore gurgled, his eyes bulged wide, then, slowly, he slipped to the floor.

Sam stood up and looked down at him. Lattimore clawed at the glass shard, trying desperately to pull it out. Then it broke off and Lattimore looked with horror at the little piece in his hand, knowing that the biggest part was still in his belly. Sam's own hand was bleeding and he realized he had cut himself as he had thrust the glass dagger into Lattimore.

"A piece of glass. Ain't this a hell of a way for Jason Lattimore to get hisself kilt?" Lattimore gasped.

"Lattimore?" the woman said in a shocked voice, looking down at him. "You're Jason Lattimore?"

"That's right," Lattimore gasped. He laughed. "Don't figure you would'a tried to help me if you know'd that."

"Help you?" the woman said, coldly. "I would have killed you myself."

Lattimore gasped one more time, then he was gone. Sam walked over to the bed and tore off a piece of the bed sheet, then wrapped it around his hand. He had just finished the make-shift bandage when the sheriff and several others came clomping up the stairs and running into the room, their guns drawn.

"Is he dead?" the sheriff asked, looking down at Lattimore.

"Yes," Sam said. He pulled out the dodger he held on the man and showed it to the sheriff. "Here's the reward poster, and there's the body. I want the money."

The sheriff looked at the dodger for a moment, then at Lattimore. "All right," he finally said. "It'll probably take a day to get it transferred to you. You got someplace to stay?"

Sam looked over at the girl, who, though still naked, had made no effort to cover herself when the others came in. She had shown spunk when she attacked him, defending the man she was with, even though she didn't know him. And she wasn't a bad-looking woman.

"Yeah," Sam answered. "If you'll get this body out of here, then get the hell out yourselves, I have a place to stay."

The woman looked up in surprise, then smiled. "Are you talking about staying with me?" she asked.

"Yeah, I guess I am," Sam answered.

"I'll just get the glass out of the bed," she said.

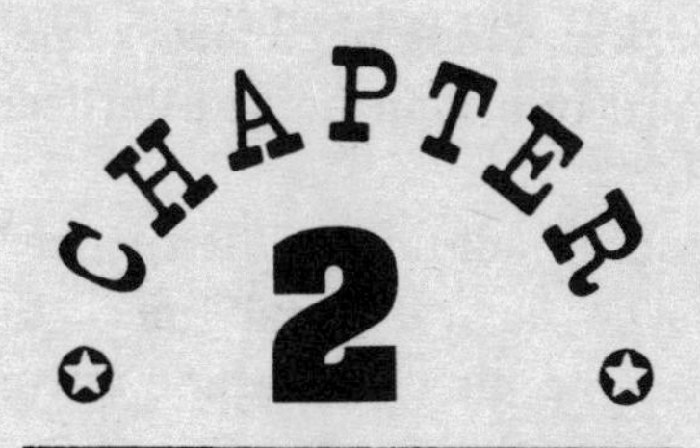

WHEN SAM STEPPED INTO THE SHERIFF'S office the next morning, the sheriff had his money all counted out for him.

"Glad you came in early," the sheriff said. "Don't much care for keepin' a whole lot of money around the place. Want some coffee?"

"Thanks," Sam answered.

"Sign the receipt there, and the money's yours," the sheriff said as he walked over to the stove and picked up the big, blue-gray coffee-pot. He poured a cup for Sam, then refilled his own cup.

"Got somethin' else for you if you're interested," the sheriff said as Sam signed the receipt.

"What would that be?"

The sheriff pulled open the middle drawer of his desk and took out a piece of paper. "You ever heard of a man named Pardeen? Henry Pardeen?"

"Yeah. Small-time cattle rustler."

"Maybe he was small-time," the sheriff said, "but he ain't small-time anymore. You know where Devil Pass is?"

"Up north some," Sam said.

"Yes," the sheriff said. "Good cattle country, lots of water and grass. Also lots of cattle rustling. So much, in fact, that when the Devil Pass Ranchers' Association heard you was down here waitin' on a reward to be paid, they came up with an offer of their own. It's in this telegram if you're interested."

The sheriff held the telegram out and Sam reached for it.

TO SAM SLATER

CONDITIONS HERE REQUIRE YOUR SERVICES. HENRY PARDEEN AND CATTLE RUSTLERS ACTIVE. CATTLEMENS' ASSOCIATION PREPARED TO MAKE YOUR PARTICIPATION PROFITABLE.

CATTLEMAN'S ASSOCIATION OF DEVIL PASS

"You got any dodgers on Pardeen?" Sam asked.

"Right over there on that table," the sheriff replied, pointing to a table against the wall. Sam walked over and started looking through the piles of wanted posters.

"If you're wantin' to know the reward, it's $250," the sheriff said. "I just looked it up this morning when I saw that telegram."

"That's not very much," Sam said, picking up the flyer himself. He looked back toward the sheriff. "I've got two or three others on my list that pay better."

"You just gonna let this one go, then?"

Sam stroked the scar on his cheek and studied the poster for a moment, then he put it down with the others and came back over to the desk to pick up his coffee.

"I don't know," he finally said. "I've got to go through that way anyway. I may as well see what they mean when they say they can make it profitable."

"I would," the sheriff agreed.

Devil Pass was a good forty miles north, and though Sam could have ridden his horse, he was temporarily flush from the reward for Lattimore, so he arranged to have his horse shipped up in the stock car, while he took a seat on the train. It was an easy way to travel and he sat looking out the window as the terrain rolled by.

The view outside wasn't anything new—rugged hills, dry sand and needle-covered cactus—but the view inside wasn't particularly attractive either, consisting mostly of overweight drummers and immigrant families, washed-out, poor and eager looking. A while back, a young cowboy wearing an ivory-handled pistol, leather chaps, and highly-polished silver rowels got on the train. He had swaggered back and forth through the car a few times, but Sam had paid little attention to him.

The scenery improved inside when a very pretty, young woman boarded the train. As she boarded, she smiled prettily, shyly, at Sam. The young cowboy in the chaps and silver rowels evidently knew her, and called her by name, Cindy, as he moved to sit near her. Sam put her out of his mind and leaned his head back, then tipped his hat down over his eyes for a little nap.

"Devil Pass! We're comin' into Devil Pass, folks," the conductor said, walking quickly through the car. Sam had been napping, and at the conductor's call he sat up and pushed his hat back, then looked around. The conductor stopped beside his seat.

"Excuse me, sir, but you said you wanted to saddle your horse before you arrived?"

"Uh, yeah," Sam said. "How far are we?"

"Just under three miles," the conductor replied.

"Thanks. If you don't mind, I'll go forward now," Sam said.

"Go right ahead," the conductor invited. "Devil Pass, folks, Devil Pass," he called. "We'll be to Devil Pass in about five minutes."

Sam got up and walked forward toward the stock car. When he stepped out into the vestibule, he saw the girl and the silver-bedecked cowboy standing on the platform between the cars.

"Please," the girl was saying. "Please, just leave me alone."

"Come on, I seen the way you was lookin' at me at the Cattleman's Ball last week. You ain't foolin' no one by playin' hard to get."

Sam had already put his hand on the door to go into the next car when he heard the exchange, and he stopped and looked back at them. He was reluctant to interfere in any discussion between a man and woman because he knew that playing reluctant was often a part of the woman's courting ritual. In this case, however, the expression on the young lady's face and the tone of her voice told him she wasn't playing a game. She was serious when she told the man she didn't want to be bothered.

"What the hell are you staring at, mister?" the cowboy asked Sam.

Sam sighed. He was just about ready to go on and leave them alone, anyway. It wasn't his business, and he generally made it a habit of not interfering in anything that wasn't his business.

"Get out of here before I get mad," the cowboy said.

Sam sighed again. Now the little son-of-a-bitch had *made* it his business.

"Why don't you go on back in the car and leave the girl alone?" Sam asked.

"What? What did you say to me?" the cowboy asked, as if shocked that anyone would even challenge him.

"I said go back in the car and leave the lady alone," Sam repeated.

"Why don't you just go to hell?" the cowboy replied, menacingly. He turned back to the girl as if dismissing Sam, but Sam wouldn't be dismissed. Sam stepped back across the gap between the two cars then, and grabbed the cowboy by the scruff of the neck and the seat of his pants.

"Hey, what the hell!" the cowboy shouted, but his words were lost in the rattle of cars and his own surprised scream as Sam threw him, bodily, off the train. The cowboy hit the downslope of the track base, then bounced and rolled through the rocks and scrub weed alongside the train. Sam leaned out far enough to see him stand and shake his fist, but by then the train had swept on away from him.

"Did . . . did you kill him?" the girl asked in a frightened voice.

"He'll be all right," Sam said. "He'll have a little walk into town, that's all."

The conductor stepped out onto the platform then, and looked around.

"I thought Mr. Wiggins was out here," the conductor said.

"Was that the fella with all the silver?"

"Yes," the girl said. "His name is Jack Wiggins."

"Was?" the conductor asked, an expression of curiosity etched across his face. "Where is he? What happened to him?"

"He decided to get off the train," Sam said.

"Get off the train? My word!" the conductor said. He leaned out over the edge of the platform, but he could see nothing. He turned to the girl.

"Miss Hardin, are you all right?"

"Yes, I'm fine, thank you," the girl said. She smiled. "Thanks to this gentleman."

"Yes, well, very well, then," the conductor said. He left them on the platform and walked back into the car.

"He called you Miss Hardin?"

"Cindy Hardin," the girl said. "My father is a rancher here."

"That cowboy work for your pa?"

"No," the girl said. "He works for Doc Solinger. I know him, but believe me, he's no friend of mine. Worse, I'm afraid he's going to be your enemy now, and he can be quite dangerous as an enemy. Please, look out for him."

"I'll be careful," Sam promised. The train started slowing then, and Sam touched his hat to Cindy. "If you'll excuse me, I must see to my horse."

"You didn't tell me your name, Mr. . . . ," Cindy called toward him.

"Sam," Sam replied. "Just Sam."

Cindy smiled. "I hope we meet again, Sam."

Sam worked his way through the train to the stock car. He began saddling his horse and had it ready by the time the train squeaked to a stop a few minutes later. When the door opened and the ramp put in place, he led the horse down, then tied it off and checked in at the Western Union office.

A small, bald-headed man was leaning over a table, writing on a large, yellow paper, as dots and dashes clicked from the instrument in front of him. After the message was finished, he clicked it a few times, then straightened up and looked around toward Sam. He pushed the green visor back from his eyes.

"Yes, sir. What can I do for you?"

"You sent this telegram?" Sam asked, showing him the telegram that had summoned him here.

The telegrapher read the note, then his eyes grew wide in awe as he looked at the man before him.

"Are you the one they call The Regulator?" he asked.

"Yeah. Now, where can I find the man who sent this?"

"Well, I sent it," the telegrapher said. "That is to say, I operated the instrument," he amended quickly. He cleared his throat. "Doc Solinger sent it."

That was the second time Sam had heard Solinger's name in the last ten minutes.

"Where can I find this Doc Solinger?" Sam wanted to know.

"He's got a ranch about two miles north," the telegraph operator said. "I'll send word to him if you'd like."

"Do that," Sam replied.

As the telegraph operator passed the word along to one of his messengers, Sam crossed the street to the hotel.

"Yes, sir," the clerk said, smiling broadly as Sam stepped up to the desk. "You'll be wanting a room?"

"The one up front, overlooking the street," Sam said, turning the book around to register.

"Oh, well, I'm sorry, sir, but I'm afraid that room is taken." He smiled. "You see, we have Mr. Bloemer, a traveling salesman who stays with us everytime he's in town, in that room. He arrived on the train not more than five minutes ago."

"Then he hasn't had time to get settled in, has he?"

"Oh, but I'm afraid he has," the clerk said. "As I say, he stays in that same room, everytime. If you'll notice, his name is already on the book."

Sam crossed through the salesman's name and wrote his own on top.

"See here!" the clerk said indignantly. "You can't do that, Mr . . . Mr. . . . ," the clerk turned the book around to look at the name and seeing that it was Sam Slater, blanched visibly. "Uh, Slater," he said. He cleared his throat. "But of course, perhaps if I could go upstairs and tell Mr. Bloemer there's been a mistake," he hedged.

"You do that."

"Of course you can have the room. That'll be a dollar-and-a-half," the clerk said.

"Charge it to the Cattleman's Association of Devil Pass," Sam instructed.

"Uh, yes, sir," the clerk said, clearing his throat again. "The Cattleman's Association of Devil Pass." He started up the stairs. "I'll just, uh, inform Mr. Bloemer of the mixup in rooms."

Sam waited patiently while Bloemer, protesting, was moved from his room. It wasn't a matter of bullying, or taking the best for himself that made Sam insist upon such an arrangement. It was a matter of survival. From the front room Sam would have a view of the whole town. If anyone was in town who represented a danger to him, he would come closer to seeing them from this room than from any other room in the hotel.

"Mr. Slater?" the clerk called down from

the head of the stairs a moment later. "Your room is ready now."

Without answering, Sam started up the stairs, his saddlebag thrown across his shoulder.

BEHIND THE BAR OF THE BOTTOM DOLlar Saloon in Devil Pass, there was a sign which read: "This is an honest gambling establishment. Please report any cheating to the management."

In addition to the self-righteous claim of gambling integrity, the walls were also decorated with game-heads and pictures, including one of a reclining, nude woman. Some marksman had already added his own improvement to the painting by putting three holes through the woman in all the appropriate places, though one shot had missed the target slightly, giving her left breast two nipples.

There was no gilt-edged mirror, but there was a real bar and an ample supply of decent whiskey. There were also several large jars of pickled eggs and sausages on the bar, and towels, tied to rings, were placed every few feet on the customers' side to provide the patrons with a means of wiping their hands.

The saloon had an upstairs section at the back; when Sam glanced up, he could see rooms opening off the second-floor landing. A heavily painted saloon girl was taking a cowboy up the stairs with her.

The upstairs area didn't extend all the way to the front of the building. The main room of the saloon was big, with exposed rafters below the high, peaked ceiling. There were nearly a dozen tables full of drinking customers, though there were card games in session at three of them.

Sam bellied up to the bar.

"What'll it be?" the barkeep asked as he moved down to Sam. He wiped up a spill with a wet, smelly rag.

"You got any good whiskey?"

"Got some Old Overholt."

"That'll do," Sam said. He slid two bits

across the bar and the bartender poured him a glass.

Sam turned his back to the bar and looked out over the room. A bar-girl sidled up to him. She was heavily painted and showed the dissipation of her profession. There was no humor or life left to her eyes, and when she saw Sam wasn't interested, she turned and walked back to sit by the piano player.

The piano player wore a small, round derby hat and kept his sleeves up with garter-belts. He was pounding out a rendition of "Buffalo Gals," though the music was practically lost amidst the noise of a dozen or more conversations.

One of the men at one of the tables got up and walked over to the bar, carrying his beer with him. There was a star on his shirt and Sam recognized him as Ev Butrum. The last time Sam saw Butrum, he was a deputy sheriff in another county. Like most sheriffs, Butrum tended to move around a lot. He was about forty, and was still good enough to handle most of the situations he might face. He was, however, a man who knew his limitations, and when he approached Sam, it wasn't with an air of belligerence.

"I was hoping you wouldn't come, Sam," he said.

"Why?"

"This isn't a simple matter of finding a man and getting a bounty," Butrum explained. "We've practically got a range war going on here between the rustlers and the ranchers. You might be gettin' yourself involved in more than you bargained for."

"Think so?"

"Yes, I do. In fact, if you was smart, you'd just ride right on out of here."

"I can't do that, Butrum," Sam said, taking a drink. "At least, not until I've heard what the Cattleman's Association has to say."

"Yeah," Butrum replied. "I figured as much. Well, if I can't talk you out of it, there's nothing I can do to stop you. Just don't say you wasn't warned."

Sometime later, in the Rattlesnake Saloon at the opposite end of town from the Bottom Dollar, Jack Wiggins stepped through the swinging doors and looked around the murky interior. Wiggins was a mess. His clothes were dirty and badly torn, there were scratches and bruises on his face, and the silver band which he wore so proudly around the crown of his hat was twisted and gouged.

Wes Murdock looked up from his table and saw his friend standing just inside the door. His eyes grew wide with surprise and he stood up so quickly that his chair fell over.

"What the hell happened to you?" he gasped.

Wiggins walked over to the table and sat down. Without a word, he reached for Murdock's beer and took several swallows. Then, looking at him with eyes flashing hate and anger, he growled, "I'm goin' to kill the son-of-a-bitch. I'm goin' to kill him the moment I see him."

"Kill who?"

"The son-of-a-bitch who threw me from the train, that's who!"

"You got throwed from the train?" Murdock asked, his eyes widening in amazement. "Who did it?"

"I don't know the bastard's name, but I know what he looks like. He's a mean, ugly-looking son-of-a-bitch, with a scar that splits his face, like this." Wiggins moved his finger across his face to indicate the scar.

"Jack, how'd somethin' like that happen?" Murdock asked. "I mean, I can't see a fella doin' somethin' like that without you killin' him."

"He caught me by surprise," Wiggins said. "I was just standin' out on the platform between cars when he come up behind me. Next thing I know, I'm bouncin' and rollin' down the side of the track and the train's goin' by, lickety split, without me."

"You was lucky you wasn't killed," Murdock said solemnly.

"Yeah, well the son-of-a-bitch that done that to me ain't goin' to be so lucky," Wiggins said. "I'm goin' to kill 'im, soon as I find 'im."

"Say, Wiggins," one of the men at the bar said. "I seen a fella that looked like that, down at the Bottom Dollar."

"Yeah? When?"

"Not more'n fifteen minutes ago. I reckon he's still there."

"Thanks," Wiggins barked. "Come on, Murdock, if you want to be in on the fun."

"Yeah," Murdock chuckled. "Yeah, I'd like that. I'd like that a lot."

Down at the Bottom Dollar, Sam was still talking to Sheriff Butrum when the bat-wing doors swung open and Jack Wiggins came in.

"Jack! What the hell happened to you?" someone asked, seeing his condition.

"Some son-of-a-bitch pushed me off the train," Wiggins said. "And I hear tell he's in here."

Everyone in the saloon laughed.

"Goddamnit! It ain't funny!" Wiggins bellowed. "I was just standin' there on the platform, mindin' my own business, when he sneaked up behind me and shoved me off."

"You weren't minding your own business," Sam said. "You were bothering a lady who didn't want to be bothered."

Sam's voice cut above the laughter and the buzz of the saloon, and it suddenly grew very quiet. Wiggins looked toward the bar and saw Sam for the first time.

"You!" he said in a choked voice. "Yeah, I was told you was in here. Pull your gun, you son-of-a-bitch! Pull your gun! I'm going to shoot your eyes out!"

There was a quick scrape of chairs and tables as everyone scrambled to get out of the way. Only Sheriff Butrum didn't move away from Sam. The sheriff looked over at the bartender, who had ducked down behind the bar.

"Fred, would you draw me another beer, please?" he asked in a calm voice.

"Sheriff, are you crazy?" Fred hissed. "Get out of the line of fire!"

The sheriff chuckled, then looked back toward Wiggins, who was standing in the doorway with his arm crooked, just above his pistol.

"Oh, you needn't worry about him," the

sheriff said, pointing to Wiggins. "He won't even get a shot off."

Several people gasped at his calm words. "Could I have that beer?"

Fred raised up just enough to take the sheriff's mug, then he drew the beer and handed it to him.

"Thanks," the sheriff said. He blew the foam off, then turned and looked toward Wiggins. Wiggins, like the others, had heard the sheriff's calm declaration, and now he was hesitating. His hand was shaking visibly.

"Wiggins," the sheriff said. He took a swallow of his beer, then wiped the back of his hand across his mouth, though he still left some foam on his moustache. "If I were you, I'd leave. You got the shakes so bad now that Slater is liable to misunderstand. He's liable to think you're goin' for your gun, when really all you're doin' is peein' in your pants."

"I'm . . . I'm not afraid," Wiggins insisted, though his voice was so choked he could scarcely get the words out.

"Where's your shadow Murdock?" Butrum asked. "I figure after this man kills you, he'll just be warmin' up. Murdock will be next."

"Hold it!" Murdock said, stepping through the door and moving to one side. He had his hands up in the air. "This here ain't my fight . . . I'm just along to watch."

"There isn't going to be anything to watch," a voice said authoritatively. "Both of you, get on back out to the ranch!"

Sam, like Wiggins and the others, looked toward the voice. A new man came into the saloon then. He was fairly small, with curly, gray hair, dark, beady eyes, a narrow mouth, and a nose shaped somewhat like a hawk's beak.

"Doc Solinger, I was just. . . ." Wiggins started, then stopped, leaving the sentence unfinished.

"You were just about to make a fool of yourself, and get yourself killed in the process," Doc Solinger said. He looked toward Murdock. "What about you, Murdock? Are you that anxious to die?"

"Not me," Murdock insisted. "I told you, I was just along to watch."

"The show's over."

Wiggins pointed to Sam. "You ain't heard the last of me, mister," he said.

"Come on," Murdock mumbled. "Let's get out of here."

Doc Solinger watched the two men leave, then turned to Sam.

"Mr. Slater? I'm Doc Solinger. I'm giving a dinner tonight for the Cattleman's Association. If you would come as our guest, I'll fill you in on what we need."

"I'll be there," Sam agreed.

As Doc Solinger promised, the Cattleman's Association of Devil Pass had their meeting with Sam over dinner in the private dining room of the Devil Pass Hotel. In addition to Sam and Solinger, there were four other men around the dinner table. They were dressed as businessmen, but most, Sam realized, would have been much more comfortable dressed exactly as he was. They were used to the saddle and to range clothes, and they pulled at their collars and tugged at their sleeves as they carved their steak and positioned their fork just so, trying to exhibit the proper manners for eating. The table had been covered with an exquisite, lace cloth and set with the finest china and crystal; the silverware and candlesticks reflected a soft, rich light.

Doc Solinger was the only one who actually seemed to enjoy the dress and formalities of the occasion. "More wine, Mr. Slater?" he offered, holding up the bottle toward Sam.

Without answering directly, Sam held his glass out to be filled again.

Solinger was more formally dressed than any of the other ranchers, wearing a three-piece suit and a silk shirt, with a diamond stickpin in his tie. He also wore a large, diamond ring and was the only man Sam had ever seen with such an affectation. As the wealthiest man in the territory, Doc Solinger was a natural for the position of president of the Devil Pass Cattleman's Association.

Other outdoorsmen might have felt intimidated by the display but Sam was neither intimidated nor impressed. However, the food was good and the drink better, and he decided that the dinner alone made it worth listening to whatever Doc Solinger and the Cattleman's Association had to say.

"I think I can speak for all the cattlemen when I say we have come to the conclusion that rather desperate measures are needed to stop the terrible plague of rustling we have been experiencing," Solinger went on.

"If this goes on any longer it's going to drive me out of business," one of the other ranchers said. He was a big man with a sweeping moustache. Sam remembered that his name was Hardin, and he figured he must be the father of the young woman from the train.

"And not only Mr. Hardin here, but me and Vogel and Masters, too," another added. This was Baker.

"Doc Solinger's the only one stout enough

to keep going," Baker went on. "In fact, when I got hit so hard last year, Doc Solinger loaned me the money I needed to make a note at the bank. If it wasn't for him, I don't know what I would do."

"At least you're tryin'," Vogel said. "Hughes and Cain just gave it up." Vogel looked at Sam. "They were in on the decision to call you in . . . in fact, it was Cain's idea in the first place. Now he's not even here to see it through."

"What happened to him?" Sam asked.

"He and Hughes are both gone," Doc Solinger said. He leaned back in his chair and sighed. "I'm afraid the truth is they were too small to even try it out here. Of course, their instinct was to fight back when Pardeen started hitting them. They didn't have anything to fight with, though. Pardeen didn't leave them enough cattle to even make all the ends meet, and they went under."

"It could've been worse," Baker said.

"How could it have been worse?" Vogel asked. "Neither one of them are here anymore."

"It could've been worse because they might have had to go back East with nothing. As it is, they at least had a little money."

"Yeah, you're right. Thanks to Doc Solinger, they didn't leave here completely broke," Vogel agreed.

"Doc Solinger bought both of 'em out," Baker explained.

"You mean you have their ranches now?" Sam asked, raising his eyebrows.

"Yes."

"I see."

"No, Slater, I don't think you do see," Baker interjected. "Doc Solinger didn't *have* to buy them out. Hell, once they abandoned their ranches the land was out there, just for the taking. Doc Solinger paid them for it, when by law he didn't have to pay them a cent."

"I couldn't just take over," Doc Solinger said. "I wouldn't have felt good about that. After all, both men did have families to support."

"He's made the same standing offer to the rest of us," Baker said. "I have to confess that knowing he will buy us out if need be, gives us a little more incentive to try and get something done."

"Which is exactly where you come into the picture," Hardin added.

"I was wondering when we would get around to me," Sam said.

Hardin took two cigars from his jacket pocket and gave one to Sam. Sam accepted, and after biting off the end, waited for Hardin to provide the match. Hardin lit Sam's first, then his own, and took several puffs before Vogel spoke up.

"Slater, you have a reputation of no-nonsense dealing with people like Pardeen and his gang," Vogel said.

"I've run across those kind of people a few times," Sam admitted.

Vogel smiled. "It's my understanding that when you do, you generally leave them dead."

"I've left my share of them dead," Sam confessed. "But they're given a choice."

"Yes," Baker interjected. "Well, Slater, we don't want these people to be given a choice. We want you to hunt them down. We want you to hunt them down, and when you find them, we want you to kill them on the spot."

Sam took his cigar out of his mouth and studied the end of it for a moment before he looked up at Baker.

"Mr. Baker, when killin' is needed, I'll kill," Sam said. "But I don't do it on command, and I'm not a professional executioner."

Baker raised his eyebrows. "You squeamish about that?"

"About killing on demand? You can say that if you want to."

"You're in one hell of a profession to be

squeamish about a little killin', aren't you?" he asked.

"Not at all. Killing is a part of my business, *if* it is necessary. Unnecessary killing is a waste of time and energy."

"If you ask me, bringing these sons-of-bitches in to be tried is a waste of the people's time, energy, and money," Vogel said.

Sam stood up and put his cigar down on the plate he had just emptied.

"You gents don't want a bounty hunter, you want an assassin," he said, quietly. "I have other things to do. You can get yourself another man."

Doc Solinger began clapping his hands slowly, as if applauding a performance.

"Bravo," he said. "Bravo, Mr. Slater." Doc Solinger smiled at the other members of the organization. "Gentlemen, if I had any doubts about Sam Slater before, I have none now," he said.

"What is this?" Sam asked.

"Well, my dear fellow, when I agreed with these gentlemen to discuss our problem with a professional bounty hunter, I had certain reservations. You will excuse me for having these gentlemen play out this little scene for you, but you must understand that I am, after all, a businessman and not a savage. I wanted to see just how far you would go. I was concerned that if we gave you carte blanche you might unleash a blood bath in our fair valley." He smiled at Sam. "But, after listening to you talk, Mr. Slater, I now believe that you are a man of integrity and ethics. Most of all, you are a man with a sense of values. I can, in all good conscience, employ your services, and know that there will not be a sudden onslaught of wanton killing. You are hired, sir."

"I'm not hired unless I say I'm hired," Sam said. He picked the cigar up again. "Now, I have a few questions of my own, if you don't mind."

"But of course you do," Doc Solinger said. "I imagine the first thing you want to know is what will be your pay?"

"That's a start," Sam agreed.

"Yes. Well, I propose that we pay you $250 for every cattle thief you eliminate by, uh, whatever method is needed, regardless of the reward that is currently in effect. In addition, you will receive whatever government award is being offered, whether more or less. And when you bring in their leader, Henry Pardeen, we will pay you $1,000. Not only that, Mr. Slater, you can begin drawing your money immediately. We are prepared to give you a $250 advance, even before the first bounty."

"The money sounds reasonable enough," Sam agreed.

"You will, of course, be required to report in to us often," Baker said. "We want to know what is going on."

"I can't do that," Sam said.

"Why not?" Hardin asked.

"You ever heard the story of putting a bell on a cat?" Sam asked. "If I have to report in here to you people, the outlaws will always have an idea of where I am. Besides, if I wanted to work for someone, I'd hire on as a deputy marshal somewhere."

"But look here! This is ridiculous," Baker sputtered. "We can't be expected to pay you this kind of money and then have absolutely no control over where you go and what you do. Worse, to not even have an idea of where you are?"

"That's the way it's going to be," Sam said.

"Of course it is," Doc Solinger said. He looked at the others. "Listen to me, gentlemen. I have more land, more cows, and more money than any of you. That means I have much more to lose than anyone else in this room, so I say we need Sam Slater. Now, if you are not prepared to employ him on his terms, I am."

There was grumbling exchange of conversation for a moment or two, then Hardin spoke up, speaking for all of them.

"All right, Slater," he said. "If Doc Solinger here is satisfied with you, then we are, too. You can operate any way you want, come and go as you like. The only thing we want is for these damn rustlers to be eliminated. Because if they aren't wiped out, and wiped out fast, there ain't goin' to be one cowman left in the whole valley."

Sam relit his cigar, smiled at them, and started for the door.

"Well? What is your answer?" Hardin called after him.

Doc Solinger chuckled. "Gentlemen, I think he just gave us his answer," he said.

IT HAD BEEN THREE DAYS SINCE SAM agreed to take the job, or at least, since the Cattleman's Association *believed* he had agreed to take the job. Of course, since he hadn't actually said anything as he was leaving the meeting, perhaps they had assumed incorrectly. After all, they hadn't heard another word from him, and two nights ago several cows were stolen from Vogel's herd. Last night the rustlers hit again, taking cows from Baker's herd.

Angered, Baker called a meeting at his house of all the ranchers in the valley.

As the nearby mountains turned from red

to purple in the setting sun, Baker's friends and neighbors began arriving for the meeting. Wagons and buggies brought entire families across the range to gather at the Baker house. Children who lived too far apart to play with each other, laughed and squealed and ran from wagon to wagon to greet their friends before dashing off to a twilight game of kick-the-can. The women who had brought cakes and pies from home, gathered in the kitchen to make coffee, thus turning the business meeting into a great social event. Many of them brought quilts and spread them out so that, while the men were meeting, they could work on the elaborate colors and patterns they would be displaying at the next fair.

The cowboys were invited, too. They had an interest in the proceedings, for if the ranchers lost their ranches, the cowboys would lose their jobs. The cowboys, however, were working hands and they didn't feel comfortable around the ranchers and their families, so most of them declined respectfully.

The Hardin ranch was one of the smallest spreads in the valley and there were only three cowboys who worked there fulltime. They were invited but had declined, and were spending the evening in the small bunkhouse. One was lying on his bunk, while the other two were sitting across a barrel head from each other, playing cards. They were playing for matches only, but that didn't lessen the intensity of their game. When one of them took the pot with a pair of aces the other one complained.

"You son-of-a-bitch! Where'd you get that ace?" His oath was softened by a burst of laughter.

"Don't you know? I took it from Shorty's boot when he wasn't lookin' a while ago." Shorty was the one lying in the bunk.

"Does Shorty keep an ace in his boot?"

"You think he don't? I never know'd him to do anythin' honest when he could cheat."

"That's the truth," Shorty answered laconically from the bunk. "But don't let Pete fool you none, Curly. He's just as bad." Pete was the dealer of the game.

"Curly cheats as much as I do," Pete declared.

"I admit I practice it a little," Curly said. "If I ever get real good at it, I'm goin' to go into one of them big gamblin' tables up in Denver an' win my fortune."

"Or get your lights put out for good," Pete replied. "Cheatin' your friends for matches is one thing. Cheatin' in a real game is liable to get a fella killed."

The cards were raked in, shuffled, then re-dealt.

"You think all them ranchers are goin' to come up with anythin' at this meeting' they got goin' on over to the Baker place?" Curly asked.

"I don't know. If they don't they're all goin' to go out of business and me an' you an' Shorty is all goin' to be lookin' for jobs somewhere."

"Maybe we could wind up workin' for Doc Solinger," Shorty suggested. "Seem's like ever'time someone quits ranchin', he takes over."

"Yeah, but if you notice, he don't hire all the cowboys from the old ranch. Hell, he don't even hire half of 'em. The rest of 'em is left out in the cold," Pete said.

"Yeah, that's true," Curly agreed.

"What I'm hopin' is that this bounty-hunter fella they hired will stop the rustlin'," Pete went on.

"One man? How can one man do that?" Shorty asked.

"This here ain't just any man. This here is Sam Slater. I reckon you've heard tell of him? He's the one they call The Regulator."

"Yeah, well, whoever he is, he's still just one man and I don't see him gettin' this rustlin' stopped," Shorty insisted.

* * *

Four riders stopped on a little hill overlooking the Hardin ranch, then ground-tied their mounts about thirty yards behind them. They moved to the edge of the hill at a crouch, then looked down toward the bunkhouse.

"Looks like they's only two of them here," one of the men said. "I can see 'em through the window, sittin' at a table or somethin'."

"The rest of them must've gone to that ranchers' meeting," one of the others hissed. "No matter, Pardeen said kill ever'one we find here, so we'll shoot both of 'em. You two, aim at the one on the left. Me and Johnny will take the one on the right."

"I'm ready," Johnny replied.

All four men raised their rifles and took slow, careful aim. Their targets were well-illuminated by the lantern that burned brightly inside the bunkhouse.

"Shoot!" the little group's leader said, squeezing the trigger that sent out the first bullet.

Pete died instantly, a bullet coming through the window to crash into the back of his head. Curly went down with a bullet in his chest. Shorty, who was on the bunk, rolled off onto the floor.

"Pete! Curly!" he called, but neither man answered.

The shooting continued for another full minute, with bullets whistling throught he window, slamming into the walls and careening off the unused stove. Shorty scooted as far up under his bunk as he could get and lay there with his arms over his head until, finally, the shooting stopped.

"Shorty!" the wounded man on the floor called. "Shorty, I'm hit. I'm hit bad!"

Shorty crawled across the floor, littered now with shattered glass from the shot-out window. When he reached Curly, he saw blood on his chest. The wound was sucking air and Shorty looked away. He knew it would soon be over.

"Who was it, Shorty? Who did this to us?" Curly gasped.

"I don't know, Curly," Shorty replied. "I don't know."

Sam was camping at least two miles away when he heard the shooting. Because of the effect of echoes, however, he couldn't be sure of the direction the shooting was coming from. He got up from his bedroll and climbed to the top of a large outcropping while the firing was still going on to see if he could pinpoint it. Then, far to the west, he saw a series of winking lights and knew they were muzzle flashes. Quickly, he began to saddle his horse.

Back at the meeting at the Baker ranch, the ranchers were complaining bitterly over the fact that rustling was still going on.

"It's time we did something about it," Vogel said.

"We did do something about it. We hired Sam Slater," Hardin replied.

"He ain't doin' nothin'."

"Give him time."

Baker held up his hands to quiet the group, then nodded toward Doc Solinger who had been watching and listening. So far, he had said nothing.

"I think maybe Doc Solinger might have a suggestion or two for us," Baker said.

At Baker's invitation, Solinger stood up to address the other men who were gathered there.

"Gentlemen, what we need," he began, "is to form a corporation. A cattle corporation."

"What do you mean?" Vogel asked.

"Yeah, how would something like that work?"

"It's really very simple," Doc Solinger said. "We would merge our ranches and our cattle into one, large, cattle company. We would each own a share of the company, in proportion with what we put into it."

"What would be the advantage of such a thing?" Hardin wanted to know.

Solinger started to answer, then he saw the woodbox sitting by the stove. Though the stove was cool now, the woodbox was full, including the smaller sticks used for kindling. Solinger reached down and picked up a few of them.

"When you're gatherin' sticks for a fire," Solinger said, "have you ever noticed how easy it is to break one stick?" He snapped a single twig. "But put several of them together, and you can't break them, no matter how hard you try." He demonstrated his point by putting several of the sticks together.

"That works with sticks," Hardin said. "But I need a more practical answer."

"All right, how about this for an answer?" Solinger went on. "Suppose you put 500 head into the corporation and 250 head were stolen. You wouldn't personally be out 250 head. You would be out only a portion of the 250 head, because the rest of us would absorb the loss with you."

"If they're his cows, why should we lose anything?" Masters asked.

"Because we'd all be partners in this

thing," Solinger answered. "We would share in each others adversity and in each others success. We would be like brothers."

"That sounds pretty good," Vogel agreed. "If you put it that way, then I'm for it."

"Yeah, me too," Masters added.

"Well, it looks like it's up to you, Hardin. What do you say?" Baker asked.

"I don't know," Hardin replied. "Most of you boys know that before I come out here, I was a cowboy, then the top-hand back in Texas. I liked workin' there and I thought my boss was the tops. But always I had it in mind to one day own my own spread. Well, I got my own spread. It's small, I admit, smaller than any of yours. But if I join up with this corporation you're talkin' about, it won't be mine at all. I'll be right back where I started, just another cowhand working someone else's ranch."

"That's not true," Solinger said. "You won't be an employee of the ranch, you'll be one of the owners, a partner in a ranch that is bigger than anything you've ever dreamed of."

"What about the men we'd need to work an outfit this large?" Hardin asked. "Where would we get them? I've only got three hands, and I do as much work as any of them."

"That won't be a problem," Solinger said easily. "One large ranch can be run much more efficiently than several smaller ones. We won't need any more men than what we already have."

"Yes," Hardin said. "But those of us who are doing a lot of our own work now will be working for the company."

"Ah, but don't forget. You *are* the company," Solinger said.

"It's well and good to say we're the company, but when it comes right down to it, somebody's goin' to have to be the boss, right?" Hardin asked. "Wouldn't a corporation have to have a president?" Hardin asked.

"Yes, of course," Doc Solinger replied. "You would have anarchy otherwise. We could make the election of a president our first priority."

"I say we elect Doc Solinger," Baker proposed.

"I agree," Vogel said.

"He's got my vote," Masters put in.

"Hardin?" Baker asked.

"I'd like some time to think about it."

"Time? Man, we're runnin' out of time! The rustlers are bleedin' us white!" Baker said.

"Excuse me, Mr. Baker?" someone said, stepping in through the door at that moment. It was one of Baker's hands.

"Yes, Goodwin, what is it?" Baker answered, still looking at Hardin as if angry with the man for refusing to go along with the others in what, to Baker at least, seemed to be the obvious solution to their problem.

"Maybe you folks better come outside here, an' look at this," Goodwin suggested.

The expression in the cowboy's voice caught the attention of the ranchers and they stopped what they were doing to step out onto Baker's front porch. Goodwin pointed toward the distant horizon, but he didn't have to. Everyone's attention had already been arrested by the orange glow of what had to be a large fire.

"That . . . that's your place, ain't it, Hardin?" Vogel asked.

"Yes," Hardin answered in a tight voice.

"Quick!" Doc Solinger said to the others. "If we get over there in time, we might be able to save some of it!"

"I've got extra buckets in the barn!" Baker shouted. "Get 'em in the wagons, men, an' let's go!"

It was quiet where Sam waited in the rocks. He could hear crickets and frogs, a distant coyote and a closer owl, but nothing else. He strained his ears in vain for the muffled sounds of approaching men, the drum of horses' hooves, the rattle of the saddle and tack. He was about to believe they wouldn't be coming this way, when, from his position, he suddenly got a glimpse of four men, silhouetted against the orange glow of the ranch they had just torched. For a moment, it was as if the gates of hell had opened and four of its most desperate tenants had escaped.

He pulled his pistol and checked his load, then waited.

The riders continued their ghostly approach, men and animals moving as softly and quietly as drifting smoke. Sam cocked his pistol and raised it.

"Hold it right there!" he called.

"What the hell?" one of the men shouted. "Who is it?"

"Shoot 'im down!" another called.

The riders pulled their pistols and opened fire. Sam returned fire and one of the men dropped from his saddle and skidded across hard ground. All hell broke loose as flashes of orange light exploded like fireballs on the rocks.

Sam was well positioned in the rocks to pick out his targets. The outlaws, on the other hand, were astride horses that were rearing and twisting about nervously as flying lead whistled through the air and whined off stone.

Sam picked out another rider and with one shot, tumbled him from the saddle.

"Where the hell is he?" one of the outlaws shouted in panic.

"Let's get out of here!" the other yelled.

Sam fired two more times, and the last two riders fell. Then it was quiet, the final round of shooting but faint echoes bounding off distant hills. A little cloud of acrid, bitter gunsmoke drifted up over the battlefield and Sam walked out among the fallen rustlers, moving cautiously, his pistol at the ready.

It wasn't necessary. All four men were dead and the entire battle had taken less than a minute.

IN THE EAST THE SUN HAD RISEN FULL disc. A dozen wagons were parked in the soft, morning light and in the wagons, nestled among quilts and blankets, slept the children of the families who had come to help fight the fire. The light of day now disclosed the damage. The Hardin house had been completely destroyed, but it could have been worse. The smoke house, grainery, bunkhouse, and barn were saved by the prodigious effort of all who had come to help.

Martha Hardin stood with her husband's arms around her, weeping softly. Cindy stood close to her parents, looking at the destruction with eyes that were wide and sad. The Hardins, like everyone else were covered with soot and ash from the blackened ruins of their home. On the ground under a tree sat a pitiful pile of the few belongings they had managed to pull from the ashes. Most of their things were burned and twisted beyond recognition, but here and there a few had survived the flames and their bright, undamaged colors shone incongruously from the pile of smoking, blackened rubble. The cast-iron cookstove stood undamaged, almost defiantly, in the midst of what had been the kitchen.

Everyone was tired and felt a great sadness for the two young cowboys who had been killed. In addition to their deaths, the destruction of a home was also particularly hard, because this was an area where homes and people were few and far between.

"How many were there?" the sheriff asked Shorty. It was the first chance for interrogation because the entire night had been passed in the unsuccessful attempt to fight the fire.

"There was four of 'em," Shorty answered.

"Did you recognize any of them?"

Shorty, who had helped fight the fire, was, like the others, covered in soot and ash. He walked over to the well and brought up a bucket of water, then took a long drink from the dipper, not yet having answered the sheriff's question. He wiped the back of his hand across his mouth, leaving a clean swipe through the soot.

"Well?" the sheriff asked again, impatient with Shorty's stalling.

"I'm not real sure," Shorty finally said. "I was hiding under my bed in the bunkhouse, remember? And besides that, it was dark. But when they set fire to the main house, it lit up the yard some, and that's when I got a pretty good look at one of them. I wouldn't swear to it, you understand, but I'm pretty sure I saw who it was."

"Who was it?" Solinger asked, coming over to join the conversation, and showing by his question that he was as eager as the sheriff to find the guilty party.

"I believe it was Johnny Robinson."

"Johnny Robinson? Are you sure?" the sheriff asked, his face plainly showing that the information was difficult for him to accept.

"Well, like I said, I don't know if I could swear to it," Shorty hedged, "but it sure looked like him."

The sheriff looked over at Doc Solinger. "Johnny works for you, don't he, Doc?"

"He did work for me," Doc Solinger

agreed, "but he doesn't anymore. I fired him about a month-and-a-half ago. He's no good, sheriff, and if I had to guess, I'd say Shorty is probably right. I wouldn't put it past Johnny to fall in with the cattle thieves."

"There's someone comin' in!" Baker called, and the men who had fought the fire all night long now stirred themselves to meet the rider.

"He's leadin' a string of horses," one of the others said. "What is it, a pack train?"

"No, look—look what's on the horses—it's bodies."

"Why, that's Sam Slater," Vogel said.

As Sam rode into the front yard, he saw the men gathering together to meet him. He stopped near one of the wagons, then climbed down from his horse, and taking his canteen from the pommel, walked over to the well to fill it. All eyes were on him—not only the men were watching but the women and children as well. The men crowded down close, the women hung back, and the children were back farther, in some cases hiding behind their mothers' skirts, peering out around them with wide, curious, and in some cases, frightened eyes.

"Slater, you want to tell us what all this is about?" Doc Solinger asked.

As Sam poured water into his canteen he

looked around at the smoking ruins of what had been the house.

"Doesn't seem like you should have to ask," he said.

"See here, Sam, are you saying these men did this?" the sheriff asked.

"Yep."

"How do you know they did it?" Baker asked.

Sam put the top on his canteen and hooked it over the pommel.

"Four of them at $250 each," he said. "I've got $1,000 coming."

"You haven't answered my question," Baker said. "How do you know these are the men who did it, unless you saw them do it? And if you saw them, why didn't you stop them then?"

Sheriff Butrum had walked over to the four horses and was checking each of the men by grabbing a handful of hair and lifting the head.

"This one is Johnny Robinson," he said. "You were right, Shorty."

"I thought I saw him," Shorty said. He walked over to look at Robinson's body, then at Sam. "I just wish it had been me instead of you that shot him. They killed Pete and Curly."

"They're just as dead, no matter who shot them," Sam said.

"Yeah," Shorty said. "I reckon they are at that."

"Mr. Slater, if you'll come into town tomorrow, I'll have a bank draft drawn in your favor," Solinger offered.

Sam remounted his horse. "I'll see you tomorrow," he said. Touching his hat as if in greeting to the ladies, he rode away from the Hardin ranch, leaving behind the gruesome cargo he had brought in.

It was late that afternoon when two riders approached the entrance to a canyon that was about ten miles northwest of the Hardin ranch. The canyon was known as Hidden Canyon, for the simple reason that it was so well concealed by the rocks and ridgelines guarding its entrance that it couldn't be seen unless someone was specifically looking for it. At the entrance to the canyon there were two tall, natural obelisks from which someone could keep a watchful eye, thus preventing anyone from approaching the canyon without being seen. Equally important, there was a source of water down inside the canyon.

These were the virtues of Hidden Canyon which caused Henry Pardeen to select it as his hideout. He had built half-a-dozen adobe shacks to house the rustlers, as well as the two or three women who had joined the group.

As the riders approached the canyon entrance they stopped, and one of them removed his hat, then waved it broadly across the top of his head, put it back on, then took it off and waved it a second time. Only then did they see the series of mirror flashes which told them they could come in.

Pardeen was told that a couple of riders were coming in, so he came outside to wait. He suffered from some rare affliction that made him almost completely hairless so that he was not only bald, but lacked eyebrows and beard as well. As a result, he looked somewhat like a cannonball. He had been eating when he heard someone was coming, so he wrapped a tortilla around some beans and took it outside with him. Some of the juice dribbled down his chin but he made no effort to wipe it off.

The riders were Jack Wiggins and Wes Murdock. Wiggins and Murdock were Pardeen's outside contacts. As cowboys for Doc Solinger, they were able to hear bits of news that they could sell to Pardeen. Pardeen knew that Wiggins fancied himself a gunfighter . . . he wore fancy, black clothes, a decorated holster, and silver gun. Pardeen had seen him shoot—Wiggins was good, but Pardeen knew what Wiggins didn't know—it wasn't just skill that made a man a good gunfighter.

Murdock, on the other hand, was Wiggins's shadow. You rarely saw one without the other, though Pardeen was never sure whether Murdock actually liked Wiggins, or was just so frightened of him that he cultivated his friendship. It was hard to imagine anyone actually liking Wiggins.

As the canyon had become not only an enclave, but a prison as well, the arrival of someone from outside always caused a crowd to gather. The rustlers drew close to hear what the two men would have to say. The women of the camp hung back, out of the way of the men, but still close enough to hear the news, any news, from the outside world. One of the women was an olive-skinned, black-eyed senorita named Rosa. Murdock once confided to Wiggins that he was particularly attracted to Rosa, though Rosa belonged to a man named Jed Kingman. Sometimes Murdock fantasized that Wiggins and Kingman would get into a fight, Kingman would be killed, and Rosa would be his for the taking. For now, he was content with long, covert looks at her. Recently, he had caught her looking back, and once, when Kingman wasn't watching, she had even smiled at him.

"What have you got?" Pardeen asked the two riders.

"You ain't goin' to like it," Wiggins said.

"Tell me anyway."

"It's about that bounty hunter, Slater," Wiggins said. "You know the Cattleman's Association hired him."

"Yeah, you told us. What else?"

"He's already earned $1,000, that's what else," Wiggins said importantly. He looked at the others, as if pleased with himself for being the center of attention. "You know the four men you sent to burn Hardin's house? Slater killed them. All four of them."

"Johnny's dead?" one of the women gasped.

"Johnny Robinson, yeah, he's one of them," Wiggins said. "He was a friend of mine, too."

"Oh, Johnny!" the woman wailed, and she wandered away crying, comforted by one of the others.

"How did it happen?" Pardeen asked Wiggins.

"Don't nobody know, really," Wiggins said. "He just showed up at the Hardin house with the bodies draped across their horses.

Ever'one was out there fightin' the fire Johnny and the others started."

Pardeen smiled. "So, they got the job done before they was shot, did they?"

"Yes."

"Good boys, they was good boys, all of 'em," Pardeen said. He smiled broadly, and rubbed his hands together. "Well, now, with all his hands dead and Hardin with no place for him an' his family to sleep, I'd say tonight would be a good night to pay a visit to his ranch. We could probably take three or four hundred head of his cows. Hell, there won't be nobody watchin', we could more'n likely take the whole damn herd!"

It was late in the afternoon of the day after the fire. The neighbors who had gathered to fight the fire were all gone now. Only Hardin, his wife and daughter, and Shorty remained behind to see to the cleanup. A wagon, its wood bleached white by the sun, sat a few feet in front of the blackened remains of the house, being filled with the ashes and burned boards to be hauled away. All four were working, but it was Cindy who saw Sam approaching.

"Here's Mr. Slater again," she called to the others.

"I wonder what he wants?" Martha said. "He frightens me."

"We got no cause to be frightened of him," Hardin said. "He's on our side."

"I'm not frightened of him," Cindy said, looking at Sam with eyes that reflected her strong attraction to him. "He came to my rescue on the train, remember? I'm not frightened at all."

Sam saw them gathered around, watching him, as he rode up. In the older woman's face he could see fear, in Hardin's, determination, while Shorty's eyes were open wide in awe. The girl was also easy to read. She studied him with a mixture of admiration and curiosity. The admiration was because Sam's features were well-formed by nature, enough to make him a handsome man. The curiosity was because nature had not been left alone.

Sam had been in too many fights, and though he had lost very few, he had, nevertheless, paid for his victories with a nose that was now mashed flat. More chilling than his misshapen nose, however, was the purple scar that slanted down his left cheek like a flash of lightning. It had been given to him by his uncle, many years ago, when Sam had moved in to stop the man from raping his own daughter, who was Sam's sixteen-year-old cousin. The uncle, a prominent rancher in Montana, had slashed Sam's face. In self-defense, Sam had fought back, killing him with his own knife.

Sam would have a scar forever.

Sam's uncle would be dead forever.

"What can I do for you, Mr. Slater?" Hardin asked.

Sam swung down from his horse and looked around for a moment, then he lay a finger on his scar and rubbed it. It was an unconscious gesture, one that he did frequently when he was more than normally aware of his scar, such as now, when the beautiful, young, Hardin girl was looking at it.

"Mr. Hardin, how many head of cattle do you have?" Sam asked.

"Don't tell him!" Martha said, quickly.

"You don't have to tell me if you don't want to," Sam replied. "But I have a feeling you won't have nearly as many tomorrow. In fact, you may not have any by tomorrow."

"Why not?" Hardin asked.

"Unless I miss my guess, Pardeen will be coming for them—tonight."

"Oh," Martha gasped.

Hardin patted his wife's hand, reassuringly, then looked at Shorty.

"Shorty, I figure you got wages comin'," he

said. "I'm goin' to pay you off now so you can get out of here."

"Are you firin' me, Mr. Hardin?" Shorty asked.

"No, not exactly. You can come back tomorrow . . . if I have any cows left. You'll still have your job if you want it, but I don't figure this is your fight, so I want you to take Martha and Cindy on into town."

"What do you mean take me into town?" Martha asked. "I'm staying out here. You can't fight them off by yourself," she protested.

"He won't be by himself, Mrs. Hardin," Sam said. "I'll be here with him."

"You? Why would you do such a thing?" Hardin asked. "It isn't your fight, either."

"Oh, but it is. The Cattleman's Association is paying me to make it my fight, remember? I'll be here when they come."

"I will, too," Cindy said.

"And me," Shorty added.

"Shorty, you sure you want to do this?" Hardin asked.

"I'm sure. I figure I owe 'em for Pete and Curly," he said. "Besides that, I put too much work in these cows just to see someone ride in and take 'em away."

Hardin smiled. "Well, that's the mark of a good foreman, I reckon."

"Foreman?" Shorty smiled broadly. "Look here, Mr. Hardin, are you tellin' me you're making' me the foreman of this ranch?"

Hardin laughed. "I reckon I am," he said. "Only thing is, right now there ain't no hands around to be foreman over. And if we don't keep Pardeen from takin' all our cows tonight, there won't be no ranch to foreman over, either."

"We'll stop him, Mr. Hardin," Shorty said. "You just tell me what you want me to do."

Hardin looked at am. "Well, I reckon that's up to Mr. Slater. Have you got any ideas, Mr. Slater?"

"Yeah, a few," Sam admitted.

"Can they wait until after we've had a meal?" Martha asked. "It's gettin' on toward suppertime; I thought I'd fix us somethin' to eat."

"I've got some jerky in my saddlebag," Sam said. He pointed to the burned-out house. "You've got enough to do without worrying about feeding me. I wouldn't want to put you out any."

"Nonsense," Martha said. "The rest of us have to eat, don't we? What's one more mouth to feed? Anyway, the stove is still here and I've just about got it cleaned up and ready to use. And the smokehouse is still full of meat. If we're going to fight a war tonight, we're goin' to do it on full stomachs."

Sam smiled. "Mrs. Hardin, you talked me into it," he said.

SAM SAT ON AN OVERTURNED BUCKET eating a supper of bacon, fried potatoes, and scrambled eggs. Hardin, who had just finished his own supper, came over to talk to him.

"You been givin' some thought to what we might do tonight?" he asked. "I mean, do you have any ideas on how to stop Pardeen?"

"Yes," Sam replied. He finished his meal, then stood up and pointed to the open end of the valley. "You're in a real good position here, Mr. Hardin. Anyone who comes for your cattle will have to come right through this draw. It doesn't look like there's any other way in, unless they come over the mountains."

"That's right," Hardin agreed. He chuckled. "And even if they could get in that way, they couldn't get nothin' back out unless they was stealin' mountain goats."

"All right, then we're going to defend this entrance. To do that, we're going to have to dig a few rifle pits," Sam said. "I want a hole over there, one over there, and another one there." The three positions Sam pointed out stretched all the way across the entrance to the narrow valley. "Anyone coming in will be under our line of fire."

"I'll get Shorty and start digging," Hardin promised. "What else will we be needin'?" he asked.

"Where is the best place on this ranch to see everything?" Sam asked, handing his empty plate to Cindy who was, at that moment, collecting the dirty dishes.

Hardin chuckled. "Well, you might ask Cindy, here, to take you to her secret lookout up on the rim," he suggested. "That is, if she's willin' to share it with anyone."

"Papa! You know about that place?" Cindy asked.

"Darlin', I been knowin' about that place

ever since you first started goin' up there, an' that was, what? Eight, ten years ago?"

"You never said anything."

"Honey, you was a young girl, bein' raised on a ranch with no one your own age to talk to except a bunch of rough, mangy cowhands. I figured you probably needed a place of your own."

Cindy smiled at her father, then walked over and kissed him on the cheek. "If I've never mentioned it, you're a good father," she said. She looked up at Sam. "If you want to have a look around we'd better go now. It'll be getting dark soon."

"All right, let's go," Sam agreed.

The setting sun, losing both heat and brilliance, was poised in the west above the desert floor. A dark, gray haze was beginning to gather in the notches of the rugged escarpment, hanging there like drifting smoke. The red, sandy loam was dotted with blue cedar and mesquite, lined in gold from the setting sun.

Sam rode along behind Cindy as they climbed the trail to her lookout. It took about five minutes of easy riding and Sam calculated that the same distance could be covered in less than two if necessary. Once there, they dismounted and Sam looked around.

"Well, this is it," Cindy said self-consciously. She moved her hand around in a sweeping gesture. "My secret hideaway."

"I can see why you like to come up here," Sam said. "It's really a nice place." He walked out on the precipice and pointed. "I figure that when Pardeen and his bunch come, they'll most likely come from that way. It's the easy way in and he'll figure that your father has either abandoned the ranch, or he's here all alone. I doubt he'll even try and sneak up on us. I'm sure that from here I'll see them in plenty of time to get back to the rest of you with the warning."

"Mr. Slater?"

"Just Sam, ma'am," Sam corrected.

Cindy smiled. "You don't have to call me ma'am," she said. "You can call me Cindy."

Sam looked at her. She was flirting openly with him now. Sometimes, he had noticed, young women tended to do that. He never really knew whether they were attracted to him out of gratitude when he helped them, or out of a sense of excitement from the danger he represented to them. Whatever the reason, he didn't like to encourage it. He had a thousand reasons why such a thing shouldn't be encouraged, none of which he was willing to share, because the very act of sharing why he couldn't be interested could, in itself, be mistakenly construed as an act of encouragement.

"Miss Hardin, when this is all over, I'll be drifting on," Sam said, quietly.

Cindy looked down at the toe of her boots. She knew he had read her mind and was telling her that she was barking up the wrong tree. And yet, she couldn't bring herself to turn away from him. She had to try, one more time, to see if there was something, down inside the man, she could appeal to.

"You know, Sam," she said, pawing at the ground self-consciously with her foot. "There's a lot of good grazing land in this valley, more than enough to support two or three families. If you were ever interested in, well, maybe in starting your own ranch, you could do worse than to do it here."

"I'm sure I could," Sam said. He looked at her for a moment, then his voice softened. "Cindy, I can't settle down here. I can't settle down anywhere. If I did, I would get homesick."

"But I . . . I thought you didn't live anywhere. I thought you were as loose as a tumbleweed."

Sam chuckled. "I am," he said. "And that's what I would get homesick for. That's the worst kind of homesick you can have."

"I . . . I understand," she said.

"I hope you do," Sam said quietly. "You're as fine a young woman as I've ever run across, and you deserve a fine man. I'm not that man."

"I guess I made a fool out of myself," Cindy said. "I'm sorry."

Sam smiled at her. "I expect in a few days I'll probably look back on this and figure I was the one who made a fool of himself," he said. He started for his horse. "We need to get back before dark. Can you shoot, Cindy Hardin?"

Cindy laughed. "I can snuff a candle at a hundred yards. Is that good enough shooting for you?"

"Good enough," Sam agreed.

Hardin and Shorty had done their work well and the three rifle pits were dug by the time Sam and Cindy came back from the precipice.

"We got the holes dug, Slater," Hardin said. "What's next?"

"Let's get settled in before they come," Sam said. "Hardin, you and your wife take this hole. Shorty, you take the one in the middle, and Cindy, you get the one over on the far side."

"Where you goin' to be?" Shorty asked.

"I'm goin' to be wandering around to wherever I figure I can do the most good," Sam said.

He smiled. "Just make sure none of you shoot me."

It was dark and quiet. A coyote howled and an owl hooted. There was the scratch of hooves on the ground and the creak of riders in saddle leather.

Hank Pardeen twisted in his saddle and stared down toward the ranch. The house was gone, but there was a single lantern burning in the bunkhouse. It seemed incredible to Pardeen that they had managed to sneak up on them without being seen, but that was just what had happened.

"Watch out!" someone said in a short, angry voice.

"Keep it quiet," Pardeen hissed. "You want them to hear us?"

"Hell, what if they do? who's here? One old man, his wife, and daughter? Even the ranch hand is gone."

"Nevertheless, keep quiet," Pardeen said. "No sense in lettin' 'em know we're here."

"They're goin' to find out pretty soon," one of the men said. He laughed a short, evil laugh. "Especially the girl. I aim to make a special point to let her know I'm here."

"Only if you beat me to her," one of the others added, and they all laughed.

"Don't be worryin' none about the girl," Pardeen said. "When I give the word, I want ever'one to shoot toward that lantern. Like as not they're all inside that bunkhouse, and small as it is, we shoot it up good we're likely to get about all of 'em. But don't shoot until we get closer and I give the word."

"Right," his men agreed.

Sam had seen the riders approaching from his position at Cindy's lookout. He rode quickly back down to the others, then ran from hole to hole, passing the word that Pardeen was coming.

"Let's hope the lantern throws him off," Sam said. "When they get close enough for you to pick out a target, shoot, but not until you're sure!" he emphasized. "Don't forget that once you shoot, you'll give away your location."

With the others warned, Sam took up his own position and waited. They were still too far away and it was too dark to make them out well enough for a shot, or even to determine exactly how many there were. Then, finally, they drew close enough. He saw them raise their rifles and aim at the lantern in the bunkhouse. His trick was working.

"Fire!" one of the riders barked.

With the muzzle flash from their rifles,

Sam had a target. He squeezed off a round, firing just to the right and slightly below one of the flashes. He heard a grunt of pain.

"They got me!" someone yelled.

"Damn? Where the hell are they?"

Sam's firing was a signal for the others to open fire as well, and Hardin, Shorty, and Cindy began shooting.

"What the hell? They been waitin' for us with a whole army!" one of the attackers shouted in a frightened voice. "We got to get the hell out of here!"

Sam heard the sound of hoofbeats as the night riders turned their horses and began beating a retreat. The defenders fired three or four more times but they were just shooting in the dark with no idea as to where their targets were. It didn't really matter—the idea now was simply to run them off, and that they had done.

"All right!" Sam shouted. "Hold your fire, save your ammunition! They're gone!"

Sam walked back toward the other pits, checking to make certain no one had been wounded. Hardin was determined, Cindy was reserved, but Shorty was excited, flushed with victory over their successful skirmish.

"We did it!" he said. "By golly, we ran them off! They won't be back!"

"Not tonight," Sam agreed. "And maybe

not to your ranch at all, but most of 'em got away and if they don't come here, they'll try somewhere else."

"There's three of 'em won't try anywhere else," Shorty said excitedly.

"Three of them," Sam said. "They're yours, Mr. Hardin. At $250 each, that's $750. You think you could rebuild your ranch house with $750?"

"Oh, no, I couldn't," Hardin said. "I wouldn't feel right trafficking in another man's death."

"Owen Hardin, don't be a fool," Martha said determinedly. "You helped kill those men, and I helped you do it. If Mr. Slater is generous enough to make this offer, I don't intend to let you refuse. If you won't take the bodies into town and claim the reward for them, I will."

"Why, Martha, I . . . I never knew you felt that way," Hardin said.

"Why not? My God, Owen, I fought off Indians with you, and wolves, and drought. If I was the squeamish kind, I would've been dead a long time ago."

"They're yours," Sam said. He started toward the barn where he had put his horse to keep it out of the line of fire.

"Where 'you goin'?" Shorty called to him.

"Out there," Sam answered without elaboration.

"But, where will you be if we need you? If this happens again?"

"Around," Sam replied.

CHAPTER 7

IN LESS THAN TWO DAYS THE VALLEY HAD been turned into a battlefield. The sudden demise of nine young men was the subject of every conversation in every bar in town, and the Rattlesnake Saloon was no exception. In fact, as Jack Wiggins and Wes Murdock sat in the back of the saloon, they could hear the excited murmurs on everyone's lips.

"The Regulator, he got four of 'em. And Hardin and his hand got three more."

"I heard that The Regulator got them, too, but then he just gave them to Hardin' to give him enough money to rebuild his house."

"Could be," someone else agreed. "I've heard he sometimes does things like that."

Wiggins listened to them. Right now, he was playing a game of Ole' Sol. Actually, he would have preferred a game of poker, but Murdock had no money and no one else would play with him, for he was always ready, at the drop of a hat, to use his guns. He was very fast and very good with his guns, and had often put on shooting displays for his fellow cowboys or the citizens of the town. Sometimes he would break bottles or snuff candles to win bar bets. His targets weren't always so innocent. Last year he killed a man in a poker game after the man accused Wiggins of cheating. Of course, Wiggins had been cheating, but he couldn't let the accusation go unchallenged. Wiggins forced the card player into drawing, so there were no charges filed against him. The story was that he had also killed a man over in Loganville for the same reason, but no one was really sure about that.

Though neither of the two men Wiggins had killed were known to be gunfighters, they were, nevertheless, victims, and that was all that was needed to enhance his reputation as a man to be avoided. What with the rustlers and night riders who were terrorizing the range, times were already bad enough. No one had any desire to add Wiggins to the growing list of dangers they must face just to survive in this rugged country.

Wiggins counted out three cards but couldn't find a play. The second card of the three was a black seven. There would have been a play had it come up on top. Unfortunately, it was one card down and therefore useless to him. Wiggins glared at it for a moment, then, with a shrug, played it anyway.

The bat-wing doors swung open and a cowboy came in and walked over to the bar. He was a working cowhand, not a gunman, and Wiggins recognized him as someone who rode for Vogel, though he didn't know his name. The cowboy ordered a whiskey, then looked around and saw Wiggins sitting at the table, calmly playing cards.

"I just come from the funerals of Pete and Curly," the cowboy said. "They was two good hands, cowmen who never did no harm to nobody, and they was shot down in cold blood."

Though the cowboy wasn't telling the people in the saloon anything they didn't already know, no one responded to his outburst. He had obviously been drinking before he came here and was in an expansive and dangerous mood.

"They was shot down in cold blood, and

the Hardin ranch, where they worked, was burned down," the cowboy went on. "But then, you was all out there helpin' to fight the fire . . . you all seen it," he said. He looked around the room, then his eyes fell on Wiggins who was still, pointedly, dealing and studying his cards. "That is, ever'one was out there but you, Wiggins. You and your shadow," he added with a derisive slur toward Murdock. "Tell us how it is that you two wasn't out there to help fight the fire at the Hardin ranch, like the rest of us?" he asked.

Wiggins looked up, nonchalantly.

"You talkin' to me, cowboy?"

"Am I talkin' to you?" the cowboy repeated. "Hell, yes I'm talkin' to you, you fancy-dressed, silver-studded son-of-a-bitch."

The others in the saloon gasped at the cowboy's careless choice of words. Wiggins, however, just smiled coldly.

"Hey, do you know who you're talkin' to?" Murdock asked, but Wiggins put his hand out to quiet him.

"It's all right, Murdock," he said. "The cowboy is just drunk, that's all. I'm inclined to let that remark pass."

"You're a lucky man," Murdock said. "He wouldn't let somethin' like that pass with most men."

"I don't want him to let it pass. I asked how come you two wasn't out to help fight the fire at the Hardin ranch with the rest of us?"

"Why should we be?" Wiggins replied. "We don't ride for Hardin, we ride for Doc Solinger." Wiggins, rifling through the cards as he talked, found another play on the table.

"I don't ride for Hardin, either. I ride for Vogel. But I was out there and so was all the other Rocking V hands. There was cowboys from nearly all the ranches in the valley, but, like I said, you two wasn't there, and I want to know why."

"He already told you," Murdock said. "We don't ride for Hardin. We got no stake in what happens to his ranch."

"Maybe that's it. Or maybe it's just that you didn't want to help put out the fire your friend Johnny Robinson started."

Wiggins looked up from the cards again. This time the nonchalance was gone. Instead, his eyes were narrowed menacingly.

"If you got something' stickin' in your craw, cowboy, I think maybe you'd better just spit it out," Wiggins said coldly.

"I ain't got nothin' stickin' there," the cowboy said. "I was only observin' that since Johnny Robinson started the fire, maybe you two wasn't in no mood to be puttin' it out. He was your friend . . . hell, ever'body knows how the three of you used to run around together all the time. I can't see that friendship breakin' up, just because he got hisself fired off the Solinger ranch."

"No law in our bein' friends with a man, is there?" Wiggins asked.

"Only the law of common sense and decency," the cowboy went on. "If I was you two, I'd be choosin' my friends a bit more careful from now on. Maybe you two are in cahoots with Robinson and the other rustlers he ran with. If you are, you better watch yourself 'cause this fella Sam Slater that the Cattleman's Association has hired don't strike me as bein' the kind of man you'd ever want to cross. He's as hard as they come and once he finds out the two of you are runnin' with the ones that's doin' all this killin' and stealin', he's likely to be comin' to ask you some questions. And if you don't want to be shot, you'd better stay out of his way. 'Course I, personally, am lookin' forward to that day."

"You keep on talkin' like this, and you ain't goin' to live to see it," Wiggins replied.

"I ain't worried. I'm goin' to be watchin' my back from now on."

"Cowboy, I don't believe I know your name," Wiggins said.

"It's Earl Peabody. Not that it makes any difference to you."

"Oh, that's where you're wrong. It does make a difference to me, Peabody. You see, me an' you are about to have us a fight."

Peabody grinned broadly. "A fight? Yeah," he said. "Yeah, there's two of you and one of me. I'd say that makes the odds about even. Come on, I think I'm goin' to enjoy this." He made his hands into fists, then held them out in front of his face, moving his right hand in tiny circles. "Come on," he said. "I'm goin' to put the lights out for both of you."

"Uh-uh," Wiggins said. "That ain't the kind of fight I'm talkin' about. I plan to make this permanent."

"You mean a gunfight? No, I ain't goin' to get into no gunfight with the likes of you," Peabody said. "Anyway, there's two of you."

"Oh, don't let that bother you," Wiggins said. "Murdock will stay out of it, won't you, Murdock?"

"Yeah," Murdock said, smiling evilly. "Yeah, this is just between the two of you. I'll stay out of it completely." He stood up and walked away, leaving the floor to the two players. Wiggins, in the meantime, stood up and stepped away from the table. He let his arm hang down alongside his pistol and he looked at the cowboy through cold, ruthless eyes. "I'll let you draw first."

"I told you, I ain't drawin' on you," Peabody said. He doubled up his fists again. "But if you'd like to come over here and take your beatin' like a man, I'd be glad to oblige you."

"I said draw," Wiggins repeated in a cold, flat voice.

The others in the saloon knew now that the cowboy had carried things too far. They knew there was about to be gunplay and they began, quietly but deliberately, to get out of the way of any flying lead.

It wasn't until that moment, seeing the others move out of the way, that Peabody began to worry that he might actually be losing control of the situation. He was still holding his fists in front of him, and he lowered them, then stared at Wiggins incredulously. "Are you blind, Wiggins? Ain't you noticed that I'm not wearin' a gun?" he asked. "If you're figurin' on forcin' me into a fight, you can just figure again, 'cause I ain't goin' to do it."

"I'll give you time to get yourself heeled," Wiggins offered.

"I told you, I ain't goin' to get into no gunfight with you."

"If you ain't goin' to fight, then get out of

here. Get out of this saloon, out of this town, and out of this valley."

"No, I ain't doin' that, either," Peabody said. "I got a right to live where I want and to say what I want." He picked up his drink, hoping by that action to show his defiance. What he showed instead was his fear, for his hand was shaking so badly that some of the whiskey sloshed over.

"You got no rights I don't let you have," Wiggins growled. "Now, you walk through that door right now, or pull a gun."

"I told you, I'm not packin' a gun."

"Somebody give him one," Wiggins said coldly. He pulled his lips into a sinister smile. "Mr. Peabody seems to have come to this fight unprepared."

"I don't want a gun," Peabody said.

When no one offered Peabody their gun, Wiggins pointed to another cowboy who was standing at the far end of the bar. The man was carrying a pistol.

"Give him your gun," Wiggins ordered. "You aren't going to be using it, are you?"

"He don't want a gun," the man said.

"Oh, I think he does."

"Listen, Wiggins, you don't want to pay Peabody any mind. He was good friends with them two boys that was killed out at Hardin's place and he's just upset, that's all. Why don't you just leave it be?"

"I said give him your gun."

"I ain't goin' to do that. If I give him a gun, you'll kill him."

"That's right."

"Well, I don't want no part of it."

"You got no choice, friend. You'll either give him your gun or you had better be ready to use it yourself," Wiggins said. He turned three-quarters of the way toward the armed cowboy. "Which will it be?"

"Now, hold it! This ain't my fight!" the cowboy said, holding out his hands to stop Wiggins from doing anything.

"Give him your gun, or use it yourself," Wiggins said again.

The cowboy paused for just a moment longer, then sighed in defeat. "All right, all right. If you put it that way, I reckon I'll do whatever you want." He took his gun out of the holster and lay it on the bar. "Sorry, Peabody," he said. He gave the gun a shove and it slid halfway down the bar, smashing through two glasses, then stopping just beside Peabody's hand. It rocked back and forth for a moment, making a little sound that in the now-silent bar seemed almost deafening.

"Pick it up," Wiggins said to Peabody.

Peabody looked at the pistol. A vein was jumping in his neck and those who were close enough to him could see his hands shaking.

"Do it," Wiggins said again.

"No, I ain't goin' to. No matter what you do, you can't make me fight."

"You think not?"

Wiggins jerked his pistol from his holster. The draw was so sudden that it looked like no more than a twitch of his shoulder before the gun was in his hand. He pulled the trigger and there was a flash of light, then a roar of exploding gunpowder. That was followed by a billowing cloud of acrid, blue smoke.

At first, everyone thought Wiggins had killed Peabody. When the smoke drifted away, though, Peabody was still standing, holding his hand to the side of his head with blood spilling through his fingers. Wiggins' bullet had clipped off about a quarter-inch of Peabody's earlobe.

"Hee-hee, ha-ha!" Murdock giggled hysterically, pointing to the side of Peabody's face.

"Pick up the gun," Wiggins ordered again.

"No."

There was a second shot and Peabody's right earlobe, like his left, turned into a ragged, bloody piece of flesh.

"Ho-ho! Hee-hee! Look at that, will you?"

Murdock said. "Ole' Jack's cuttin' him up like a can of kraut!"

"Pick it up!"

"No!"

Wiggins sent his third bullet crashing into Peabody's kneecap. Peabody shouted out in pain, then bent over to grab his shattered knee.

"You're crazy!" he said.

"You got another knee," Murdock chortled. "Don't give up yet, you got another knee!"

"Pick up the gun," Wiggins said, calmly.

Peabody stared at Wiggins through fear-crazed, hate-filled eyes. Then, suddenly, the fear left his eyes. They became flat and void, as if he had already accepted the fact that he was a dead man. He had one emotion left, and one emotion only: absolute, blind rage. He let out a bellow that could have come from a trapped mountain lion, or a banshee from hell.

"I'll pick it up!" Peabody yelled at the top of his voice. "I'll pick it up and I'll blow your brains out, you low-assed, no-count, son-of-a-bitch!" He made a mad, desperate grab for the gun, knocking over the whiskey bottle in the process.

Wiggins watched, allowing a slow smile to play across his face. He waited patiently until Peabody had the gun in his hand and cocked before he drew again. This time his bullet caught Peabody in the neck and Peabody, surprised by the suddenness of it, dropped the gun unfired, and clutched his throat. He fell back against the bar, then slid down, dead before he reached the floor.

Wiggins looked around the saloon, a broad smile on his face. "Well, so much for the loud-mouthed Mr. Peabody," he said. "Anyone else have anything to say?"

Everyone studied their glass or bottle, avoiding Wiggins's eyes.

"Anyone plannin' on sayin' it was anything other than a fair fight?" Murdock challenged. "I'm a witness, I saw everything. Anybody plannin' on disputin' my testimony?"

The sound of the gunshot brought two or three outsiders into the saloon, including Sheriff Butrum. He saw Peabody sitting down against the bar, his eyes open and sightless, his hand clenched tightly around the unfired pistol.

"Oh, hell," Butrum said quietly. He looked over at Wiggins. "Did you do this?"

"Look in his hand, sheriff," Murdock said. "If Jack hadn't shot him, he would've shot Jack."

"Is that the way it was?" Butrum asked the others. When no one answered, Butrum asked the bartender directly. "Fred, is he calling it right?"

"You heard what Murdock said," Fred replied.

"You know Murdock. Wiggins could lie and Murdock would swear to it. I can't count him as a credible witness. Now I'm asking you. How did it happen?"

"Peabody wanted to kill him," Fred said.

"Then you agree with Murdock? You're saying it was self-defense?"

Fred looked at the others in the bar but, as before, none of them would return his gaze. No one seemed willing to comment.

"Yeah," Fred mumbled. "It was self-defense."

Butrum looked at Wiggins. "I got the idea this ain't quite what it looks like."

"Well, now, sheriff. Are you callin' me a liar?" Wiggins asked. "'Cause if you are, I reckon you're goin' to have to back it up."

"If I have nobody to dispute your word then I have no legal right to doubt it," Butrum said. "But I don't have to like it." He sighed, then looked toward a couple of Rocking V hands. "He belongs to you boys," he said. "Take him over to Prufrock's. I'll come along to make the arrangements."

The two cowboys picked up their fallen

friend and carried him out the door, followed by the sheriff.

"Ha!" Wiggins said after the sheriff left. "Did you see how he backed down?" He whipped his gun out and spun the cylinder. "He knew better than to tangle with me, yes, sir." He waved the gun around the room and as it passed, the men either ducked, pointedly, or averted their eyes. Wiggins laughed again, then he put the gun away.

"Yeah," Murdock said. "They knew better than to tangle with you, Jack."

"Where's Anne?" he asked, referring to one of the girls who worked the bar, plying the customers for drinks and offering sexual favors for a little extra. For some reason, the killing had left Wiggins sexually stimulated.

Anne, the girl he asked for, was behind the piano. She ducked her head, hoping she wouldn't be seen, but Wiggins found her.

"Ah, there you are," he said. "Come on, let's you and me go upstairs for a while. I got me a need that only you can fill."

"What about me, Jack?" Murdock asked. "You want me to wait here for you? I'll wait if you want me to. You know me, Jack. I'll do anything you say."

"No, you don't need to wait here," Wiggins

said. "You go on back out to the ranch. I'll see you later."

"Yeah," Murdock said. "Yeah, I'll see you later."

"Me an' this girl got some business to tend to," Wiggins said. "Her kind of business," he added, grabbing himself, then laughing boisterously at his own joke.

Anne, hiding her fear behind a practiced smile, led Wiggins toward the stairs. Murdock, knowing then that he was about to be left alone, suddenly realized that he had better leave so he scooted through the bat-wing doors just as Wiggins and the girl disappeared upstairs.

IT WAS A GOOD HALF-HOUR LATER WHEN Sam came in for a cold beer. He noticed the bartender's hands shaking as he put the beer before him, but that was nothing new to him. Men often shook when he was around them . . . Sam Slater seemed to have that effect on people.

All conversation in the saloon had stopped when Sam first came in, but when everyone saw that he had nothing in mind beyond nursing a quiet beer, the talking resumed. Just by remaining silent and listening to what was being discussed, Sam learned that a cowboy named Peabody had just been killed by Jack Wiggins. Wiggins, Sam remembered, was the young man with all the silver that he had thrown from the train. He was a rider for Doc Solinger, so Sam figured it was a difference of opinion between a couple of cowboys. It had nothing to do with the rustling, and therefore, nothing to do with him.

The bar patrons were so caught up in the excitement of their conversation that they weren't even aware that Sam was around. He liked it that way. He was too private a man to actually want or need friends, but neither did he like it when everyone cringed in fear.

A girl came down the stairs and went up to the bar. When Sam looked over at her, he noticed that one eye was red and swollen.

"My god! What happened to you, Anne?" the bartender asked.

"Nothing," the girl said, putting her hand up to cover the eye.

"Don't tell me nothing. You've got as big a shiner there as I've ever seen on anyone."

"He . . . he wants a bottle of whiskey," Anne said, putting some money on the bar.

"What happened to you? Did Wiggins hit you?" The bartender reached up to touch Anne's eye, but she pulled away from him.

"No, please, Fred," Anne said. "I don't want any trouble."

"Honey, it looks to me like you've already got it. What's going on up there? Listen, you want me to go tell him his time is up?" Fred started toward the stairs.

"No, don't!" Anne said. "It's all right, nothing is going on." She reached out to grab him. "Nothing, honest. Please, leave it alone. You saw what he did to that cowboy."

"Honey, you don't have to go back up there," Fred said. "Not if he's beating you."

"It'll be all right," Anne insisted, taking the whiskey. "I just don't want any more trouble, that's all."

Anne started for the stairs, but by the time she reached the bottom step, Wiggins, wearing only his trousers and gunbelt, appeared at the railing on the upper balcony.

"Hey, you! Bitch!" he shouted down at the girl. "I sent you down there to get a bottle of whiskey, not to have a quilting bee. You've been down there long enough. Get back up here!"

"Wiggins, she's already been up *there* long enough," Fred said.

"What do you mean, she's been up here long enough?"

"Well, you know how it is," Fred answered,

forcing a laugh. "I mean, Anne's a working girl. There's other gents in here wantin' her time, too. I can't let one man just have all her time. Why, how'd it be if you was waitin' on her right now?"

"Yeah? Well, I ain't waitin' on her," Wiggins said. "But I want to be fair about it," he added with a mirthless smile. He looked down over the floor of the saloon. "Who's waitin'?" he asked. "Who else wants her?"

Anne looked out over the floor, her eyes showing an expression of desperate hope that someone would back up the bartender.

There was absolute silence. The men who were already adept at avoiding Wiggins' gaze now managed to avoid Anne's eyes as well.

"Well, now, that's just what I thought," Wiggins said. The smile left his face. "There ain't nobody but me want her, 'cause she's nothin' but a worthless slut. Now, you get back up here."

Anne shut her eyes tightly, squeezing out a tear. She started up the stairs, then she stopped. She clenched her hands into fists and shook her head resolutely.

"No," she said. "No, I'm not coming back up."

"What do you mean you ain't comin' back

up? I paid for you, by god! You hear me, girl? I paid for you! You belong to me."

"Your time is up," Anne said.

"My time is up when I say my time is up."

Anne put her hand in a dress pocket, then pulled out two pieces of silver.

"Here's your money," she said. "I'll give it back to you."

Wiggins pulled his pistol and pointed it toward Anne.

"I don't want my money, bitch. I want you. Now you get back up here or else I'm goin' to put a bullet right between your eyes."

"Miss, if you're not busy now, I'd like a little of your time," Sam said. He had stayed out of it until now. If the girl had been dumb enough to voluntarily go back upstairs, then he wasn't going to try and stop her, but if she didn't want to go up, he was just feeling contrary enough to see to it that she didn't have to.

Wiggins looked toward Sam, then recognized him. His face twisted into a grotesque smile.

"Ah, if it isn't The Regulator," he said. "What are you doing in town, Mr. Slater? I thought you were out hunting down rustlers."

"I thought I might have a drink," Sam said. "And maybe spend a little time with a woman."

"Yeah? Well, not with this woman. She's comin' back up to me."

"I don't think she wants to do that, and, as a matter of fact, I don't want her to do it either."

"What the hell do I care what she wants?" Wiggins said. "She's got no choice. Neither do you, mister. Or, haven't you noticed that I happen to be holding a gun in my hand?"

"Oh, yeah, I see the gun," Sam said. "But what are you going to do with it?"

"What do you mean what am I going to do with it?" Wiggins answered, obviously exasperated by Sam's question.

"The gun is pointing at the girl," Sam said, "but she's not your problem, I am. If you move it toward me, I'm going to kill you. If you shoot her, I'm going to kill you. If you so much as twitch, I'm going to kill you. The only way you are going to get out of this alive is to drop your gun right now."

"What? Are you crazy?"

"What'll it be, Wiggins? Are you going to drop the gun, or are you going to die?"

With a shout of rage, Wiggins swung his gun toward Sam and fired. The bullet slammed into the bar just alongside him. In one motion, Sam had his own gun out and he fired back just as Wiggins loosed a second shot.

Wiggins's second shot smashed into the mirror behind the bar, scattering shards of glass but doing no further damage. Wiggins didn't get off a third shot because Sam made his only shot count.

Wiggins dropped his gun over the rail and it fell with a clatter to the bar floor, twelve feet below. He grabbed his chest, then turned his hand out and looked down in surprise and disbelief as his palm began filling with his own blood. His eyes rolled back in his head and he pitched forward, crashing through the railing, then turning over once in mid-air before he landed heavily on his back alongside his dropped gun.

Wiggins lay motionless on the floor with open but sightless eyes staring toward the ceiling. The saloon patrons who had scattered when the first shot was fired, now began edging toward the body. Up on the second floor landing, a half-dozen girls and their customers, in various stages of undress, moved to the smashed railing to look down on the scene.

Gunsmoke from the three charges merged to form a large, acrid, bitter cloud which drifted slowly toward the door. Beams of sunlight became visible as they stabbed through the cloud. There were rapid and heavy footfalls on the wooden sidewalk outside as more people began coming in through the swinging doors. Sheriff Butrum was one of the first in.

"What the hell, Fred? Am I going to have to move my office into here? This is the second killing in here today."

"Yeah," Fred said. He pointed to Wiggins's body. "But this time it's different. This time the son-of-a-bitch needed killin'."

Seeing that the dead man was Jack Wiggins, Sheriff Butrum smiled broadly. "Yeah," he said. "Yeah, you're right." He looked over at Sam, who had already put his gun away and was leaning against the bar. "I won't ask if you're the one who did it," Butrum said. "I figure you're the only one could of."

"It was a fair fight, sheriff," Fred said. And, whereas before, the others in the bar had been deadly silent when Sheriff Butrum had solicited information, this time they were all willing to testify.

"Damndest thing I ever saw, sheriff. Wiggins already had his gun out," one of the witnesses said.

"You need someone to give a statement, I'll be more'n willin' to," another added.

"I don't reckon I'll be needing any," the

sheriff said, smiling at Sam. "I'm not even goin' to ask any questions about this one."

By now all the bar patrons had gathered around Wiggins's body and a few of the more curious were even squatting beside it to get a closer look.

"Where you reckon all his silver is?" one of the men asked.

"More'n likely still up in the girl's room," another answered.

"Sheriff, I'll get his boots and belt buckle," Fred said. "If he has any family anywhere, it ought to go to them."

"I don't know that anyone would claim the likes of him," Butrum said. "More'n likely, that stuff will bring just about enough money to get him buried." He sighed and stroked his chin, then pointed to two of the bystanders. "You two men get him over to Prufrock's hardware store so he can get started on a coffin for him. That is, soon as he finishes the one he's workin' on now."

"We'll take him over there, sheriff, but if this keeps up, I'm thinkin' old Prufrock is goin' to have to start puttin' people on."

The two men Butrum assigned to the job picked up the body, one under the shoulders, the other at the feet. Wiggins sagged badly in the middle and they struggled to carry him. A couple of the other patrons held open the swinging doors while the two men carried him out into the street.

"Gentlemen," Fred said after the body was outside. "This calls for a celebration. Drinks are on the house."

The patrons hurried to the bar and Fred happily began pouring. Butrum walked over to Sam and nodded at the happy throng.

"Hell of a note, isn't it, when a man's death is cause for a celebration?"

"I've got a feeling that people like Wiggins would rather go out this way than not be noticed at all," Sam said.

"You're probably right," Butrum replied.

"Mr. Slater, I want to thank you for what you did," Anne said, coming up to him then.

"It needed doin'," Sam replied.

"Anytime you want to stop by and see me, you're more than welcome," she added in what was an obvious invitation.

"Thanks," Sam said, though he made it plain by the tone of his voice and the way he leaned against the bar that he had no intention of taking her up on her offer . . . at least not now. With a wan smile, the girl walked back toward the piano, and a moment later, found someone else to engage her time.

"I'd better get back to the office," Butrum

said, setting his empty beer mug on the bar. "See you around."

Sam nodded, then turned back to nurse his drink in solitude. With the body gone and the excitement over, most of the customers soon returned to their own tables to discuss the shooting. It was compared with the earlier shooting, then played and replayed a dozen times over. Once or twice a couple of the men made some small comment to Sam, but for the most part, he was left alone. And that was just the way he wanted it.

THAT EVENING THE CATTLEMAN'S ASSOciation met in emergency session. Solinger had the floor.

"I know there were many who didn't like him, but Jack Wiggins was a good man. He'd been with me for two years . . . he was almost like a son to me. And now he's dead, shot down by the very man we hired to protect us."

"My god, Solinger, you can't really be sorry to see him gone, can you?" Vogel asked. "Why, not half-an-hour earlier, he killed one of my best men, practically in cold blood."

"The report says it was a fair fight," Solinger replied.

"To hell with the report. Everyone said what they thought he wanted them to say because they were afraid of him. Now that he's dead the true story has come out. Wiggins forced the fight."

"Maybe so, but it was a fight between young, hot-blooded men, and it had nothing at all to do with the problem of rustling. Don't you see what I'm getting at?"

"No, I don't think I do."

"What I mean is, this fight may very well have happened whether Slater was here or not. It was part of the natural order of things. But Slater killing Wiggins wasn't." Solinger ran his hand through his hair. "I don't know, I feel responsible, somehow. I mean, I brought Slater in here and what has it done except create an atmosphere of killing? Why, do you realize that since he arrived there have been eleven killings? Eleven men dead in just a few days," he said.

"What did you expect, Solinger?" Hardin asked. "Did you expect the rustlers to leave, just because we hired The Regulator?"

"I don't know," Solinger replied. He put his hand to his forehead and sat down in his chair. "I don't know what I expected. But I didn't plan on starting a bloodbath." He looked over at Vogel, then sighed. "And as for your hand, you have my sincerest sympathies," Solinger replied. "I truly regret Mr. Wiggins's part in that unfortunate incident. I suppose I have too much faith in human nature. I nurtured the hope that one day he would stop pretending to be a gunfighter and turn into a productive citizen."

"For god's sake, Solinger, the man had already killed two people before he shot Peabody. He wasn't *pretending* to be a gunfighter. He *was* one."

"Yes, as much as I hate to admit it, I suppose he was. Still, he was one of my own, so I plan to bury him in the cowboy's cemetery out on my ranch."

"What about you, Vogel? Where are you plannin' on buryin' Peabody?"

"In Boot Hill tomorrow, just after noon," Vogel said. "We don't have a cemetery out at the Rocking V, but I'll be lettin' all the boys off to come into town for the funeral. I've already paid for the coffin and took care of the preacher. He's all set to read over the body."

"Me an' my boys'll be there," Masters said.

"So will we," Baker added.

"Yes, I imagine most of us will be. But, gentlemen, if you don't mind, I'd like to suggest that we get back to the topic of our discussion," Solinger said. "As you know, I am concerned about the bloodshed we've unleashed in our valley and I have a question for this group. Which do we value more? Is it property, or the human life?"

"What are you gettin' at?"

"I think it's about time we faced up to our responsibilities. A killing fever has been spread over the land and I believe Sam Slater is the one who brought the fever to us."

"You know, gents, Doc may have a point," Masters said. "When you think about it, we were a pretty peaceful town until Slater come along. Ever since he arrived there has been a lot of killing."

"Okay, but let's look at it," Hardin said. "Surely you aren't saying that the four men who burned my ranch didn't deserve killing? Or the three who were killed when they attacked my place that night?"

"Or Jack Wiggins, for that matter," Vogel added.

"Those are the only deaths Slater is responsible for and as far as I'm concerned, it's good riddance to all of them."

"And the rustlin' has stopped," Baker added. "You've got to consider that. At least, I haven't lost any more cows."

"None of us have," Hardin admitted. "They're afraid to come out at night because they know Slater's out there, just like a night hawk, waiting to pounce on them from the dark."

"I know how you men feel," Solinger said. "Hell, if you remember, I was as much for hirin' him as any of you. But now, I'm beginning to wonder if we did the right thing."

"So, where does that leave us?" Masters asked.

"That leaves us with a decision to make," Solinger said.

"Hell, if you're trying to figure out whether or not we should keep him, then I say, let's bring it to a vote. But if we're going to vote, I'm telling you here and now, I'm going to vote for him," Hardin said.

"I am, too," Vogel said. "I have to admit that the killing does bother me and I think we should keep an eye on it. But, so far, he hasn't killed anyone who didn't force it on him. So, for now, I'd say let's keep him around."

"Sorry, Doc, but I'm afraid I'm going to have to vote for him to stay," Masters added.

"Me, too," Baker said.

"Doc?" Hardin asked. "You're the only one we haven't heard from.

Solinger sighed. "All right, I suppose I'll

vote to keep him, too," he agreed. "I just hope we aren't making a big mistake."

Hardin smiled. "Then it's unanimous. Sam Slater stays on the job."

Sam Slater was unaware that the Cattleman's Association was conducting a meeting to decide his fate. Even if he had been aware, he would have been unconcerned. He was a man with a singleness of purpose and his purpose was to break up the rustling ring and bring in Pardeen. He was going to do that now, regardless of whether or not he had the endorsement of the Association.

Though he still had a room in the hotel, he found that he was actually spending most of his nights out on the prairie. That was because the people he was chasing did most of their work at night, and if he wanted to catch them, he had to be out there with them. He was, as Hardin had indicated, a night hawk.

On this night he killed a rabbit and cooked it over an open flame for his supper. It was during his meal that he realized he was being watched. Slowly, showing no sign that he even knew anyone was out there, he extinguished the fire and spread out his bedroll as if he were about to go to sleep. He was careful to place his boots at the foot of the bedroll, and his hat at the top. After that he crawled down into the blanket, lay there for a moment, then in the darkness, silently rolled away and slid down into a small gulley nearby. Pulling his pistol, he cocked it as quietly as he could and inched back up to the top of the gulley to stare through the darkness toward the bedroll.

From here, with his boots and hat in position, it looked as if someone were in the blankets, sound asleep. Sam smiled in grim approval. If his campsite looked that way to him, it would look that way to whoever was dogging him.

He waited.

Out on the prairie a coyote howled.

An owl hooted.

A falling star flashed across the dark sky.

A soft breeze moaned through the mesquite.

And still he waited.

Almost a full hour after Sam had "gone to bed," the night was lit up by the great flame-pattern produced by the discharge of a shotgun. The roar of the shotgun boomed loudly, and Sam saw dust and bits of cloth fly up from his bedroll where a charge of buckshot tore into it. Had he been there, the impact debris would have been bone and flesh rather than dust and cloth, and he would be a dead man.

Instantly thereafter, Sam snapped a shot off toward the muzzle flash, though he was just guessing that was where his adversary was, as he had no real target.

"Oh, you son-of-a-bitch! You're a smart one, you are," a voice shouted, almost jovially. The voice was not near the muzzle flash and Sam knew that his would-be assailant must have fired and moved. Whoever this was, he was no amateur.

Even as Sam thought this, he realized that the assailant could use the flame pattern from his own pistol as a target, so he threw himself to the right, just as the shotgun roared a second time. Though none of the pellets hit him, they dug into the earth where he had been but an instant earlier and sent a spray of stinging sand into his face. Sam fired again, again aiming at the muzzle flash, though by now he knew there would be no one there. A moment later he heard the sound of retreating hoofbeats and knew that his attacker was riding away.

Who was it? Who was after him?

As Murdock approached the entrance to the Hidden Canyon the next day, he stopped to remove his hat, then waved it broadly across the top of his head. A moment later he saw a flashing mirror, indicating that he could proceed. When he reached the innermost part of the valley, he saw the bull-like man with a bald head and a heavy, hairless brow waiting for him.

"Hello, Pardeen," Murdock said, swinging down from his horse. "Surprised to see me?"

"No," Pardeen answered. "I heard about Wiggins gettin' his fool self shot down. I figured you couldn't make it without 'im, so I been lookin' for you."

"It's okay if I stay, ain't it?" Murdock asked anxiously. "I mean, I don't have to go back or anythin'?"

"I guess you can stay," Pardeen agreed. "But I got to tell you, you was a lot more valuable to us on the outside than you are in here. Besides which, you ain't goin' to like it too much in here."

"That's all right," Murdock replied. "I don't figure I'll be in here all that long before we have everything took care of. Anyway, don't forget that we still got someone out there, lookin' out for our interest."

"I'm not likely to," Pardeen said. "Come on, get down and have yourself a cup of coffee. We've got some plans to make."

Murdock walked over toward the fire where a large, blue-steel coffeepot hung by a wire. He picked up a chipped and stained cup, bumped the dust out of it, then tipped the pot over to pour a stream of thick, black liquid. As he raised the cup to his lips and blew on the steaming coffee, he looked around.

"Where's Rosa?"

"Rosa?"

"Yeah, you know the one. Big, black eyes? She was Jed's girl."

"Oh, yeah, I know the one you mean," Pardeen said. "She's over there, by that kettle. Don't know why you're interested, though. She's still cryin' over Jed gettin' hisself killed the other night."

"I know. But she's goin' to need someone to comfort her. It might as well be me." Even as Murdock spoke, Rosa caught his glance and smiled coquettishly back at him. "See what I mean?" he said, starting toward her.

"Yeah, well, you're goin' to have to take care of that later," Pardeen said. "First, we got us a little job to tend to, and as long as you're goin' to be here with us, you're a part of it."

"What is it?"

Pardeen chuckled. "We're goin' to pay a visit to the Rocking V," he explained. "I figure we'll drop in along about noon when everyone on the ranch is in town at the cemetery, buryin' that cowboy Wiggins shot. There won't be a livin' soul left out at the ranch. We can just ride in and help ourselves to as many cows as we want to drive away."

Murdock chuckled. "Yeah," he said. "Yeah, that's a good idea. I got to hand it to you, Pardeen. Takin' them cows is goin' to be as easy as takin' candy from a baby."

CHAPTER 10

THE SUN WAS HIGH OVERHEAD AT THE Rocking V ranch, a brilliant, white orb fixed in the bright, blue sky in such a position as to take away all the spots of shade where the cattle would normally congregate. With the shade denied them, the cows had all moved down to mill about Stillwater Creek. Stillwater Creek was the stream of water that made the Rocking V a ranch instead of a stretch of barren desert. Some of the cows had come to water, while others were there just to be nearer the band of green grass that followed the stream on its zigzagging path across the otherwise brown floor of the valley.

The main building and outhouses of the ranch sat empty under the midday sun. Everyone on the ranch, Vogel's family and all his hands, had gone into town for Peabody's funeral. Peabody had been a man who never made more work for others by shirking his own responsibilities. As a result, he had been well-liked by everyone who knew him. As if it were out of respect for him, the ranch was quiet, with even the dogs and chickens maintaining their silence.

Pardeen was right when he said that every hand on the place would be in town for peabody's funeral. He was wrong, however, when he said there wouldn't be a soul on the place. Sam Slater, anticipating exactly what Pardeen had in mind, was waiting for them. He was standing on a rock, sucking on the sweet root of a stem of grass, when he saw Pardeen, Murdock, and two others come riding in, moving across the valley floor as leisurely as if they had all day to accomplish their job.

It would be easy, Sam thought, to set up an ambush. From this angle and range he could use his rifle to cut down at least two of them before they even knew they were in danger. If he acted quickly enough he would be able to shoot them, then take out the remaining two before they had time to get away. Sam knew that there were some bounty hunters who would do just that.

But though Sam would kill when killing was needed, he wasn't the kind of man who would dry-gulch his quarry. Instead, he decided to take the more humane, though admittedly less sure, method of confronting them and offering them a chance to surrender. He swung into the saddle, then rode toward the stream where nearly a hundred cows were watering. Here, he was protected from observation by a long finger of ridgeline which ran parallel to Stillwater Creek.

"How many are we goin' to cut out?" Sam heard one of the rustlers ask.

"Well, they's four of us. We should be able to drive 'em all . . . at least the ones that's right here," another answered.

"You know, this beats it, though. I mean, I went into this business in the first place 'cause I didn't want to punch cows, and what am I doin'? I'm punchin' cows."

The others laughed, then one of them answered, "Yeah, but our cut is a dollar a head for ever'one of these cows we move. You know any cowboys who are makin' that kind of money?"

"No, I reckon not."

They were close enough now that Sam could hear them quite clearly. That meant they were close enough for him to confront, so he slapped his legs against the side of his horse and crested the ridge. There, no more than twenty yards in front of him, he saw the four riders getting ready to move in on Vogel's cows.

"Why don't you fellas just hold it right there?" he called.

"What the hell? Where'd you come from?" Pardeen hissed, startled by Sam's sudden appearance.

"That doesn't matter," Sam said. "Shuck your guns and raise your hands. We're goin' into town."

Suddenly there was an angry buzz, then the sound of a heavy bullet tearing into flesh. A fountain of blood squirted up from the neck of Sam's horse and the animal went down on its front knees, then collapsed onto its right side. It was almost a full second after the strike of the bullet before the heavy boom of a distant rifle reached Sam's ears.

The fall pinned Sam's leg under his horse. He also dropped his pistol on the way down and now it lay just out of reach of his grasping fingers.

"What the hell? Who's that shooting?"

Pardeen shouted, pulling hard on the reins of his horse who, though not hit, was spooked by the sight of seeing Sam's horse go down. "Is it one of our men? Who is it?"

"Who the hell cares?" Murdock shouted back. "Look at him! Slater is pinned down. Here's my chance to kill the son-of-a-bitch!" He raised his gun and fired at Sam.

Though Sam's right leg was still pinned, he was able to flip his left leg over the saddle and lay down behind his horse, thus providing him with some cover. Murdock's bullet dug into his saddle and sent up a little puff of dust, but did no further damage.

"Shit!" Murdock said. "I can't get to him from his angle."

"Come on!" Pardeen called. "Let's get the hell out of here while the getting is good!"

"Not until I put a bullet in Slater!" Murdock insisted. "I still owe the bastard for what he did to Wiggins." He slapped his legs against the side of his horse and moved around to get a better shot at Sam.

Sam made one more desperate grab for his pistol but it was still out of reach. His rifle, however, was in the saddle sheath on the side of the horse which was on the ground and Sam could see about six inches of the stock sticking out. He grabbed it and was gratified to see that it could be pulled free. He jerked it from the sheath and jacked a shell into the chamber, just as Murdock came around to get into position to shoot him.

"Goodbye, Mr. Regulator," Murdock said, raising his pistol and taking careful aim. The smile left his face as he saw the end of Sam's rifle raise up, then spit a finger of flame. The .44-40 bullet from Sam's rifle hit Murdock just under the chin, then exited the back of his head along with a pink spray of blood and bone as Murdock tumbled off his horse.

"He got Murdock!" one of the men said.

"That's his own damn fault. Let's get the hell out of here!" Pardeen shouted.

Pardeen and the two men with him were riding away hard now, not even bothering to look back to see what happened to Murdock. In the meantime, another bullet whistled by from the distant rifle. When Sam located the source of the shooting, he saw a mounted man with one leg thrown casually across his saddle. Using that leg to provide a stable firing platform, the shooter raised his rifle to fire again. There was a flash of light, the man rolled back from the recoil, then the bullet whizzed by so close to Sam's head that it made his ears pop. All this before the report of the rifle actually reached him. With a gasp of disbelief, Sam realized that this man was firing from at least 1,000 yards away! Sam fired back, not with any expectation of actually hitting his target, but merely to show his enemy that he wasn't completely helpless.

In a way, Sam was running a bluff, because he *was* practically helpless. He was still trapped under his horse and he knew if he didn't get himself free soon, whoever was shooting at him would be able to change locations and catch Sam in an exposed position. Sam tried again to pull his leg free but he was unable to do so. Then he got an idea. He stuck the stock of the rifle just under the horse's side and grabbed the barrel. Using the rifle as a lever, he pushed up and wedged just enough space between the horse's flesh and the ground to allow him to slip his leg free.

His first fear was that his leg might be broken, but as soon as he pulled it out, he knew that it wasn't. The blood circulation was cut off, however, and when he tried to stand he promptly fell back down again. As it was, that turned out to be a blessing, for another bullet whistled by at that very moment, at the precise place where his head would have been had he been standing.

Crawling on his belly, Sam slithered and twisted his way down to the stream. He reached the bank, then got down into the water just as another bullet ploughed into the dirt beside him. Sam twisted around behind the bank and looked back up toward the place where the shots were coming from. With the stream bank providing him cover and a rifle in his hands, he was no longer a sitting duck. Whoever was after him realized this as well, for Sam saw him put his rifle back in the saddle sheath, then turn and ride away as casually as if he were riding down Main Street. And why not? There was no way Sam was going to hit him at this distance, at least, not with a .44-40 Winchester.

After the rider was gone Sam managed to capture Murdock's horse, which had trotted away during the shooting, but afterward wandered back to begin cropping grass. Sam needed Murdock's horse to replace the one that the long-distance shooter had shot out from under him. Once he was mounted, he rode up to the top of the distant ridge to the spot where the shooting had come from. He wanted to have a look at the place where the gunman had been.

A flash of sunlight led him to the first sign. When he picked it up he saw that it was the brass casing of a .45 caliber shell of a type made especially for the Whitworth. The Whitworth, Sam knew, was a hexagonal-shaped, long-barrel rifle which, when fitted with a telescope, could be fired accurately at ranges up to 1,000 yards. It had been the preferred weapon of the long-distance sharpshooters during the War Between the States.

There weren't very many such guns, but Sam knew someone who used one—Evan McAlister. Evan McAlister liked to use the Withworth for long-distance shooting. Another interesting thing about McAlister that Sam could remember was that when he was up close he preferred the sawed-off shotgun to a pistol. The man who had come after him in his bedroll had used a shotgun. Could his would-be ambusher that night have been Evan McAlister? And was that same Evan McAlister the one who was firing at him today from a thousand yards away?

It had to be, and yet, if so, why? Nothing else fit the pattern.

Evan McAlister was a bounty-hunter who normally ranged quite a bit farther north than this. He was also a man who went for the big payoff and a sure thing. If this was McAlister, why was he after Sam? Sam *did* have paper out on him, but that was up in Montana, and as far as Sam knew, the reward on him wasn't high enough to interest someone like McAlister to come after him. Especially in view of the fact that Sam was anything but a sure thing. If it was McAlister, why was he after Sam? And if it wasn't McAlister, who was it?

Laying that puzzle aside, Sam rode back down to where Murdock's body lay sprawled in death. He picked the rustler up, threw him across the saddle pommel, then rode into town with him.

Boot Hill was located at the western end of town. Wagons and buggies were leaving the cemetery as the friends of Earl Peabody began returning to their own lives as Sam rode into town.

"That's twelve," someone said quietly as he saw Sam ride by with Murdock's body drapped across his horse. "Twelve men have been killed since The Regulator arrived in town."

Sheriff Butrum stood on the little, wooden sidewalk just in front of his office as Sam flipped Murdock's body off his horse. Murdock landed on his back, sending up a little cloud of dust. Several people were nearby and a few of them came over to stare curiously at the body. His eyes were open and glazed, there was a small, black hole just under his chin, and a much larger one, with blood-matted hair, at the back of his head.

"Why, this here is Murdock," someone said.

"He was Wiggins' shadow, remember? You never seen Wiggins without also seein' Murdock."

"It's Murdock," word went on down the street. Within moments, others were coming toward the sheriff's office, anxious to get a look at the latest victim of the rapidly escalating death toll.

"You sort of wasted your time with that one, didn't you, Sam?" the sheriff said. "Murdock's no rustler. He rides for Doc Solinger."

"Not since yesterday, he didn't. He *was* ridin' for Doc Solinger, but after Wiggins got hisself killed, Murdock quit," someone in the crowd said.

Doc Solinger pushed his way through the crowd and looked down at Murdock's body, then up at Sam.

"What'd you shoot him for? He was as harmless as they come. Why, without Wiggins to tag along after, I doubt this boy could even go to the bathroom by himself."

"This 'boy' as you call him, tried to kill me. I killed him in self-defense. I had no choice."

"Why, he was afraid of his own shadow. It's hard for me to picture him throwing down on anyone, especially someone like you," Solinger said in a voice that indicated he didn't believe Sam. "What do you suppose would make him do such a thing?"

"Let's just say that he found himself in what he thought was an advantageous position," Sam explained. "Turns out he was wrong."

"I see. Uh, Mr. Slater, perhaps it's about time we had a little talk. Just you, me, and the Cattleman's Association." Looking around, Solinger saw Vogel, Hardin, Baker, and Masters in the crowd, and nodding at them, he invited them to be a party to the conversation.

The Cattleman's Association had its office next door to the sheriff's office. The office had been closed during Peabody's funeral and the men had to wait for a moment while Doc Solinger unlocked the door. Once inside, they took their usual seats around the table, with Doc Solinger in his position at the head, as the Association's president. As the office had been closed up for most of the day, it was quite hot and stuffy. One of the men raised a window to let in some air, and with the air, came the odor of horse-droppings from the street. To most of the townspeople the street odors were as unnoticeable as the other odors of the town . . . the rotting garbage, the stale beer and whiskey from behind the saloons, the several dozen outhouses which reeked in the mid-day sun. To someone like Sam, who was used to the wide-open spaces, the smells of civilization were overpowering.

Doc Solinger took out a handkerchief and wiped his face, then pointed to a chair, inviting Sam to be seated. Sam declined, leaning instead against the wall. He took out the makings and started rolling a cigarette.

"Is there a problem?" Sam asked, leaning against the wall.

The others looked at Solinger, not only because he was the head of the Association, but because he was the one who had called the meeting.

Solinger drummed his fingers on the table for a moment, then answered Sam's question.

"Yes, Mr. Slater, there *is* a problem. We've already had one meeting to discuss the situation and events are dictating that we have another. I have to tell you that we of the Association, as well as many of the citizens of the town, are becoming quite concerned with what seems to be an excessive amount of bloodshed since your arrival. Every reward that the Association has paid so far has been paid for a body. Not once since you arrived, have you brought in a living prisoner for reward. That, despite the fact that the reward is just as high for those you bring in alive, as it is for those you bring in dead."

"I haven't killed anyone who wasn't trying to kill me," Sam said. "And they have all been rustlers . . . the very people you are paying me to hunt down."

"What about Wiggins?" Baker asked. "And Murdock? They weren't rustlers."

"I don't know about Wiggins. But I killed Murdock on Vogel's ranch."

"So, what are you trying to tell us? That Murdock, who has no history of cattle rustling, suddenly decided to become a rustler?" Solinger asked.

"You don't think they were planning to borrow Vogel's cattle, do you?" Sam replied.

"Damn!" Vogel said, slamming his fist into his open hand. "Slater's right, Doc. It all makes sense. Of course the bastards would choose today to come. They knew that all of us would be at the funeral."

"But Murdock?"

"He must've gone with them," Vogel said. "Hell, you said it yourself. Murdock wasn't the kind of man who had the gumption to do anything on his own. Hell, he could be led around like a little puppy dog."

"Just because a man lacks gumption, that shouldn't be enough cause to get him shot,"

Solinger said. "And I think we should discuss it."

"I don't," Hardin said.

"What do you mean?" Solinger asked, surprised by the comment.

"Doc, this is the second time you've called a meeting about this," Hardin said. "Now, we voted to keep him the last time and I'm willin' to bet we're going to vote to keep him this time. The truth is, I'm gettin' tired of holdin' a meeting everytime someone gets themselves shot. I say he's doing a good job and I say let's leave him alone."

"I agree," Baker said, and Vogel concurred.

"Am I the only one worried about the excessive amount of killing going on around here?" Doc Solinger asked.

"As far as I'm concerned, it's not excessive as long as it's needed," Hardin said.

"But are we sure that it's needed?"

"We don't have any reason to believe that it isn't."

Doc Solinger sighed and leaned back in his chair. He pressed his hands together and studied Sam for a long time before he spoke.

"Very well, we'll keep you on, Mr. Slater. However, for my own peace of mind, could I have your assurances that no more people will be killed?"

"I'm sorry, but I can't promise that," Sam said.

"Then can I have your word that no more will be killed than is absolutely necessary?"

"I've already given my word on that," Sam said. "I see no reason to do it again."

"He's right, Doc," Hardin said. "I told you, let's just leave him alone and let him go about his business."

"I agree with Hardin," Masters said.

"Vogel? Baker?"

"I think he's doing a bang-up job," Vogel said.

"He's got my vote," Baker added.

"All right, all right, I'll go along with the majority." Solinger agreed. "But I want it clearly understood that I am on record as abhorring all the violence which I believe this man has spawned."

"We'll keep that in mind," Hardin said.

"Is that all?" Sam asked.

"Yes. I'm sorry, Mr. Slater. We won't be calling you in again."

"Good."

"All I have to say is, keep up the good work," Vogel said. "If you hadn't been on the job, I would have lost a sizable part of my herd."

"Yeah. I guess we owe you an apology and our thanks," Baker suggested.

"I'm not interested in your apology or your thanks," Sam said. "What I'm interested in is my $250."

"BEANS AGAIN!" ONE OF PARDEEN'S MEN growled, as the fat, Mexican woman spooned them onto his plate. "Is that all we ever have around here?"

"We habba no more beef, senor," the cook said. "And the bacon, she is gone, too."

"Well, now, this is a hell of a note, ain't it?" the man complained as he walked over to sit at the rough-hewn table with half-a-dozen other men. "I mean we've rustled enough beef to start a full-sized stampede, but we ain't got so much as a mouthful of meat to lay alongside our beans."

"Quit your bellyachin'," Pardeen growled as he held his own plate out. "If you want meat for every meal, you can always go back to punchin' cows for $30 a month. You're rustlin' cows because it pays more, not because it's an easy life."

"Perhaps you ain't noticed it lately, Pardeen, but we ain't exactly been rustlin' a hell of a lot of cows, either. In fact, it's been quite a while since we've so much as took one steer and got away with it."

"Yeah," one of the other men put in. "You said it'd be a piece of cake to go out to Hardin's place and take his herd. Well, we went out there and we lost four men burnin' the place down and another three when we raided the ranch. They was good men, too, ever' one of 'em. All that and for what? We didn't get so much as one cow."

"And we didn't get nothin' from the Rocking V, either, except one more man got hisself killed."

"You mean Murdock? He wasn't worth a tinker's damn anyhow. Who cares about him?" Pardeen replied.

"Whether he was worth a tinker's damn or not don't matter. What matters is, we went out there to take some cows and we didn't get none. Instead, we met up with a bounty hunter who killed Murdock and run the rest of us off with our tails between our legs."

"Yeah, this here fella they call The Regulator has just about brought our rustlin' days to a halt."

"It don't seem right that one, ordinary man could do that to us."

"The Regulator ain't exactly what would you call an ordinary man."

"What do you mean?"

"He's more like a ghost than a regular man. I mean, no matter where we go, he's there first . . . comin' in as silent as smoke, raisin' hell, then goin' away without so much as a scratch for all the shootin'."

"He's just been lucky so far, that's all."

"Lucky, hell. Luck ain't got nothin' to do with it. I've heard of him before. They say that Sam Slater is the very best there is, and I'm here to tell you, he ain't no ordinary man."

"You've run into him, Pardeen. What do you think?" one of the men asked their leader.

Pardeen spooned some beans onto his folded tortilla, then took a bite and chewed thoughtfully before he answered. "What do I think?" he repeated "I think we need to kill the son-of-a-bitch. That's what I think."

"Easy enough to say, not so easy to do.

Sam Slater ain't the kind of man that dies easy."

"Bullshit. Put a bullet in his hide and he'll die just like ever'one else," Pardeen growled.

"Then how come we ain't been able to kill him?"

"We haven't tried," Pardeen said. "Except for Wiggins and Murdock, and they don't count for much because one of them was a blowhard and the other was a damn fool."

"Are you sayin' that *you'd* be willin' to go up against him?" one of the men asked Pardeen.

"Hell, no," Pardeen answered. "I ain't willin' to go up against him and I don't figure anybody else should have to, either."

"What do you mean? I thought you said he needed killin'."

"He *does* need killin'," Pardeen said. He smiled. "But what does goin' up against him have to do with it? What the hell, we don't need to make no sportin' contest out of this. We ain't like Wiggins, tryin' to be known as the 'Fastest Gun In The West'. There don't none of us need to try it alone, and there ain't no need to face the son-of-a-bitch down. I mean, all that's needed is for someone to kill the bastard. If he's shot in the front or in the back, it don't make no difference. He'll be just as dead."

"Yeah," one of the others said. "Sneak up on the son-of-a-bitch and shoot him in the back. That's the way to handle him."

"I got an idea how maybe to get this done," Pardeen said, wiping some of the dripping bean juice from his chin. "S'pose we all put $100 in a pot, just like as if we was playin' poker. If one man kills Slater, then all the money is his. If more than one does it, then they'll split up the money."

"Yeah, that sounds like a good idea," one of the men said. He stuck his hand into his pocket and pulled out a wad of bills. "Ante up, fellas. I don't need anybody to help me, the way I'm goin' to it. And if I am the one that kills Mr. Sam Slater, then I want to see how much money I'm goin' to get."

Some fifty miles away from the outlaw's valley and an equal distance from Devil Pass, Evan McAlister was just approaching the town of Cactus Needle. The sun was down and the night creatures were calling to each other. A cloud passed over the moon, then moved away, bathing the little town that rose up before him in silver. Two dozen buildings, half of which spilled yellow light onto the ground out front, faced the town's single street. The biggest building at this edge of town was the livery stable, dark inside, though lighted outside by the town's only street lamp. The most brightly lit building was the town saloon.

McAlister stopped his horse at the edge of a little stand of cottonwood trees and ground-hobbled him. He pulled his long-barreled Whitworth from the saddle sheath, then unwrapped the specially oiled cloth he kept around it. The hexogonal barrel gleamed in the moonlight as McAlister opened the breach and slid in the long, conical cylinder that made up the bullet and casing to which the rifle had been adapted from its original ball and cap mechanism.

Evan McAlister was only 5′2″ tall and weighed just under 130 pounds. Despite his size, he rode a very large horse, the big black stallion standing at least two hands higher than average. The result of this unlikely combination was to make McAlister look even smaller and his horse even larger than it actually was.

In New York, where McAlister grew up, his diminutive size had been quite a disadvantage. Strength and the ability to uses one's fists were what established the hierarchy of McAlister's neighborhood. Bullied by those who were larger than he, McAlister's earlier years were shadowed by intimidation and shame. Then one day in desperation, Evan McAlister grabbed a shotgun and blew a hole in the guts of one of his tormentors.

No one else in the neighborhood had ever seen an argument settled by any means other than sheer strength. When they saw the strongest of their number brought down by the weakest, they were visibly frightened and gave McAlister a new and unexpected respect.

McAlister discovered two things about himself that day: he had no compunction about pulling the trigger and he liked the feeling of power he experienced by seeing others cowering before him. It was a feeling he didn't intend to surrender, ever again.

However, one didn't just shoot his tormentor in New York without answering to the law. McAlister had to flee the city and when he did, he came West. It was the best thing to ever happen to him. Here he learned that he was actually an excellent marksman with the long gun. Soon after that he discovered a trade that would allow him to use his newly developed skill. He became a bounty hunter, specializing only in the most desperately wanted men, the "Dead or Alive" cases. This way he could kill without compunction or fear of punishment, and also be paid for it. It was as if the avocation had been developed especially for him.

McAlister developed a great pride in his craft, and like any craftsman, had the desire to be regarded as the best. Though McAlister was highly regarded, the name most revered was the one whose tracking abilities, trail skills, and other attributes combined, made him the undisputed best. In fact, he was so good that although bounty hunters were often referred to as regulators, only one was The Regulator. That was Sam Slater, and Sam Slater was definitely a thorn in Evan McAlister's side.

Then, almost a year ago, McAlister ran across some wanted paper on Sam Slater. The idea was very tempting. He could legally get rid of his biggest competitor and make a little money, too.

The reward for Sam Slater was $1,500. That wasn't bad for a normal case, but, of course, Sam Slater wasn't a normal case. In the first place, the reward was posted by a county sheriff in Montana. Even if McAlister killed Slater and even if he could prove to the Montana sheriff that he had killed him, it might be difficult to get his money. Besides, the risks involved in getting rid of Sam Slater were worth a lot more than the mere $1,500 he would be paid if he were successful.

McAlister decided, reluctantly, that it

wasn't a job he was ready to undertake. However, he did keep the circular with him . . . just in case. Then, a couple of weeks ago, the conditions changed drastically. McAlister was offered $7,500 to kill Sam Slater. Seventy-five hundred dollars was a lot of money and the circular he was carrying meant that the job would not only be legal, but might also provide him with a $1,500 bonus.

McAlister accepted the offer. So far he had made two attempts at Slater and had missed both times. He was going to try again, but not just yet. He needed to back away a bit, to give Slater time to let his guard down again. McAlister was most effective when the element of surprise was on his side.

The gunman had a most unique way of operating his business. He called it "running a trap line." By putting out the proper bait, he could reasonably expect his quarry to show up in one of his traps.

The saloon in Cactus Needle was one such trap. Through his network of paid contacts, McAlister had let out that an accomplice was needed for an easy payroll robbery. Anyone interested in the job was to walk out of the saloon at Cactus Needle at exactly nine o'clock in the evening on this very day, come to the lamp post by the stable, and examine his pocket watch.

That would be the signal by which they would meet. Further arrangements would be concluded at that time.

Earlier today, McAlister learned that someone had, indeed, taken the bait. It was Arnold Fenton. Though Fenton had been small-fry up until now, he had killed a bank teller during his last hold-up and was now worth $1,000 dead or alive. For someone like Evan McAlister, collecting that $1,000 would be as easy as picking an apple from a tree.

Inside the saloon, Arnold Fenton stood at the bar nursing a beer. He had come in with just enough money for a beer and a plate of beans. He wished he had enough money to go into the backroom with one of the two women working the bar, but he didn't. He didn't even have enough money for a second beer. If everything worked out though, that would soon change. Fenton was here to meet a man to plan a job. After that his pockets would be full again. He looked over at the wall clock.

"Is your clock right?" he asked the bartender.

The bartender, who was busy polishing glasses, set the towel down and pulled out his watch. He flipped open the case and looked at it, then glanced back at the clock.

"Yes, sir," he said. "It is lacking five minutes of nine o'clock."

"Thanks," Fenton replied.

"Would you like another beer, sir?"

"No, thank you. Not just yet," Fenton answered.

"Very good, sir."

The bartender went back to wiping glasses. Fenton raised his nearly empty beer mug, just enough to wet his lips.

According to the instructions, Fenton was to go outside and stand under the street lamp in front of the livery at exactly nine o'clock and examine his pocket watch. He didn't actually have a pocket watch—he had sold it long ago—but he figured if he pretended to be examining one it would amount to the same thing.

He took another swallow of beer, then made a face. He had been nursing the beer so long that it was now flat. It was pure hell to be in this world without money. He looked back toward the wall clock and saw the minute hand move to one minute until nine. He finished his beer, slapped the mug down, wiped the back of his hand across his mouth, and started for the door.

"Come again," the bartender called to him.

"When you've got more money," one of the bar girls called. She followed her chiding with a high-pitched laugh. The man with her guffawed in a rich, bass tone.

"I will," Fenton replied.

I will like hell, he thought. When he had enough money he was going to go someplace where he could have a good time . . . someplace like Denver or San Francisco. He wouldn't be caught dead in a place like this.

McAlister held a match to his watch face and saw that it was ten minutes to nine. He figured that was close enough to the time that it wouldn't be necessary for him to check it anymore. All he would have to do was wait for his man to show, and that should be any time now.

A man came out of the saloon and stepped into the street. He stood there for a moment looking in both directions. McAlister raised the rifle to his shoulder and waited. The man looked back toward the saloon and shouted something, then another man came out and the two of them walked together toward the opposite end of the town, away from the stable.

McAlister lowered the rifle.

Behind him his horse whickered and stamped its foot.

Somewhere down in the little town, a dog barked.

A back door slammed shut in one of the

houses, and in the moonlight McAlister saw a man heading for the toilet, carrying a wad of paper with him.

From the saloon he heard a woman's high-pitched laugh, then the lower guffaw of her companion.

A mule brayed.

Another patron came out of the saloon, and like the first man, stood for a moment on the street, looking both ways. McAlister watched him carefully, then saw him start toward the stable. Again McAlister raised his rifle and pointed it toward the street lamp.

The man stopped under the light of the lamp post, reached into his pocket, then raised his hand to study it pointedly. McAlister aimed at the easy target the street lamp provided for him, squeezed the trigger slowly, and was rocked back by the recoil of the exploding cartridge. Even from here, he could see part of the man's skull fly away as the heavy lead slug crashed through his head.

The heavy boom of the shot rolled back from the distant hills so that it sounded almost like a volley, rather than one, exceptionally well-placed shot. McAlister mounted his horse and rode quickly toward the sprawled body of the man he had just shot. By the time he reached the stable more than two dozen townspeople had poured out of the saloon, the closer houses, and other buildings, to gather around the body.

"Who did this?" someone was saying. "Did anybody see anything?"

McAlister saw a glint of light on the questioner's chest and realized it was the reflection of a star. This was the sheriff of Cactus Needle.

"I did it, sheriff," McAlister said, swinging down from his horse.

"You?" the sheriff said. His eyes narrowed as he took McAlister in, a small man dressed in black, riding a big, black horse with a long rifle sheathed on one side, and a sawed-off shotgun on the other. He recognized him almost at once. "You're McAlister, aren't you?"

"That's right," McAlister said. Though he had never let on to anyone, he enjoyed being recognized. More than that, he enjoyed the fear such recognition often instilled in people, even someone as hardened as this sheriff.

"Who is this man?" the sheriff asked.

"His name is Arnold Fenton," McAlister said. "There's a $1,000 reward out on him. Dead or alive," he added pointedly. He nodded toward the hotel. "I'm going to take a room in the hotel for tonight; I expect you'll have verification and payment by noon tomorrow, won't you?"

"Yes, sir," the sheriff said. "I'm sure I will, Mr. McAlister."

"Thank you."

"Mr. McAlister, how far away were you when you made that shot?" someone asked from the crowd.

"If you go back to that stand of alamo trees, you'll find the empty shell casing," McAlister answered.

"My god, that's over 500 yards away . . . in the dark," someone said in awe.

"I'm goin' to get me that shell casin'," a young boy shouted, and his declaration set half-a-dozen other young boys in motion, all scampering to be the first to lay claim to the souvenir.

"That there is about the most feared man in the West," McAlister heard someone say as he started toward the hotel. He swelled with pride.

"Next to The Regulator, that is," another commented, correcting the first.

"Yeah," the first man replied. "You're right. Next to Sam Slater. Can't nobody hold a candle to Sam Slater."

McAlister was a little miffed at first, then he smiled. Let them think whatever they wanted for now. After he took care of Sam Slater, they'd change their tune.

* * *

Back in Devil Pass, Sam had answered a summons to come to the Hardin ranch.

"What do you think?" Hardin asked, pointing to the new house. "Of course, it don't have nothin' but a canvas cover for a roof, but by the time we get a roof on it'll be as fine as the old one ever was."

"It'll be even better," Martha said, beaming proudly. "I was hoping to get the old house fixed up, or maybe even get a new one. Of course, I never planned on getting it this way," she added.

"You got it built pretty fast," Sam said.

"That's the way it is out here when neighbors get together," Hardin said. "Mostly it was the Association."

"Ah, yes, the Association," Sam said.

"They've been pretty hard on you, haven't they? I apologize for that."

"It comes with the territory," Sam replied.

"Nevertheless, they're coming at you like the Spanish Inquisition or something," Hardin said. "They have no right to question your methods or your motives."

"I appreciate your kind words," Sam said.

"Words? Humph. Words are a dime a dozen," Martha replied. "We want you to eat dinner with us."

"I'd be mighty pleased," Sam agreed.

Dinner was fried chicken, mashed potatoes, fresh butterbeans, biscuits, and gravy. It was topped off with a large slice of apple pie.

Shorty ate with them. He apologized and explained that as he was the only hand remaining, he had taken to eating with the family. Martha said he was almost like one of the family anyway, and Sam noticed in the exchange of glances between Shorty and Cindy, that he might, indeed, be a part of the family some day.

"Pa," Cindy said after the dessert was finished. "Can we show him now?"

Hardin smiled. "Sure, I guess now's as good a time as any," he said. "Mr. Slater, if you don't mind, I'd like you to come on out to the barn with us. Cindy and Shorty have something they want to show you."

Puzzled, Sam followed Hardin and the others outside. Shorty went into the barn, and came back a moment later leading a big, black horse. The horse, which was already saddled, was a magnificent animal, with a coat so lustrous that the sunbeams that playing off him danced in flashes of blue lightning.

"You'll be needin' a horse to replace the one that got killed," Hardin said.

"Yes," Sam agreed. He pointed to the

horse he had ridden out on. "I rented this one from the stable."

"What about this one?"

Sam went over to look at the horse more closely. He was a perfect horse with flared nostrils and eyes that flashed fire.

"You like him?" Cindy asked Sam.

"He's about the best-looking piece of horseflesh I've ever seen," Sam said, patting him on the neck. "How much are you asking for him?"

"He's not for sale," Hardin said.

"What? But I thought . . ."

"He's yours," Cindy interrupted. "A gift to you from us."

"No," Sam replied. "I can't do that. I can't take him for nothing."

"Sure you can," Hardin insisted. "Martha, Cindy, Shorty, and I have already discussed it and we figured we owe you something for what you did for us . . . not only helping us fight off the raid, but also in letting us claim the reward. You got your horse killed, you need another one, and we want to give this one to you."

"He's a good one," Shorty said. "I raised him myself from a colt. I was going to make him a part of my string, but I think you'll have better use for him."

"Get on him, see how it feels," Hardin suggested.

Sam swung up into the saddle, then leaned down and patted him on the neck a couple of times.

"Go ahead," Shorty said. "Give him a run. I want you to see what you've got."

"All right," Sam agreed. "I'll just do that." He slapped his legs against the horse's sides. "Let's go," he said.

The horse burst forward like a cannonball, reaching top speed at once, surprising Sam by its immediate response. Sam bent low over his withers, feeling the rush of wind in his face and experiencing the pure thrill of the run, feeling almost as if he and the horse were one, sharing the same muscle structure and bloodstream. The horse's hooves drummed a rapid rhythm against the ground, kicking up little spurts of dust behind them. When Sam pulled him to a stop and turned him around a moment later, he was amazed at how far he had come in such a short time. As he returned to the little group in front of the barn, he had a big grin on his face.

"What do you think?" Shorty asked.

"I have to tell you, this is more horse than I've ever been on before."

"You'll take him, then?" Cindy asked, anxiously.

"Miss Hardin, right now I believe I'd fight anyone who tried to take him away from me," Sam replied.

"He's yours," Hardin said. "Come inside, I'll give you a bill of sale."

"I've never given him a name," Shorty said. "So you can call him anything you want."

Sam smiled. "He doesn't need a name," he said. "There's just the two of us. He knows who he is and I know who I am."

THREE DAYS AFTER SAM KILLED MURdock, he uncovered what he had been looking for—he found the valley where the rustlers were hiding out.

Actually, he was pretty sure of its location even before he found it, because he had already looked in every other valley and draw within thirty miles of Devil Pass, and this was the only place left that it could be. Then, when he started exploring this canyon and saw that it had a narrow, easily guarded entrance, he knew he was in the right spot. After that there was nothing for him to do but dismount and let his new horse crop grass while he sat in the shade and kept watch for a while.

It was mid-afternoon when two riders finally exited the canyon. One was tall and lanky with a bushy, walrus-type moustache. The other was short and stocky with a scraggly beard.

"Well now, I thought you might show up sooner or later," Sam said under his breath. He recognized the riders as the two men who had been with Pardeen and Murdock. He moved out to a ledge overlooking the pass, then lay very still as they rode right beneath him. He was so close that he could hear them as they were talking.

"I tell you, Zeke, we ought not to be doin' this. Pardeen ain't goin' to like it much, us ridin' out on our own," the short, stocky rider said.

"He'll calm down when we bring in a side of beef," the tall, lanky one answered. "Come on, Quinn, admit it. Ain't you gettin' damn hungry for somethin' more'n beans and tortillas? Wouldn't a little beefsteak go good now and again?"

"Yeah," Quinn replied. "It would. But I still don't know if this is such a good idea. I mean, plannin' a job on our own."

"What job?" Zeke replied. "This ain't no

job. I mean, we ain't really goin' out to do any rustlin' or anything. We're goin' to find one cow, that's all. And we ain't even goin' to drive it anywhere. We're goin' to butcher it on the spot and we're goin' to bring back the choice pieces. We'll be back before sundown and have beef in our bellies before we go to sleep."

The two men continued their conversation, but they rode out of earshot so that Sam was no longer able to follow what they were saying. It didn't matter. He didn't have to hear any more, for he had already heard enough to realize that they were acting on their own, and that no one else would be coming out behind them.

Sam hurried back to his horse, mounted, then rode parallel with the two riders while also making a very big circle so as not to be seen by Zeke and Quinn. He put his horse into a ground-eating gallop and easily raced ahead of them. Then, a few minutes later, he suddenly appeared on the trail just ahead of the two riders. Startled by his unexpected appearance, both horses reared and Zeke and Quinn had to fight them to bring them back under control. Sam sat there calmly, patting his own horse on the neck so that it wouldn't become excited by the antics of the other mounts.

"Good evenin', boys," he said easily.

"Son-of-a-bitch, it's Slater! Where'd you come from?" Quinn shouted. Once he had his horse under control, his shoulder jerked as if he were about to go for his gun, but Sam shook his head and cocked the pistol he was already holding in his hand. The metallic sound was cold and frightening, and it stopped Quinn before he made a mistake.

"I wouldn't," Sam said.

Quinn let his arm drop by his side.

"There. That's more like it," Sam said. "The two of you undo your gunbelts and hand them to me."

Quinn and Zeke did as they were ordered.

"Thanks," Sam said, hooking the gunbelts across his saddle pommel.

"What do you want with us?"

Sam waved the barrel of his pistol in a motion to indicate they should get going. "I want you to come with me," he said. He smiled. "You're money in the bank, don't you know that?"

It was nearly sundown by the time Sam herded his two prisoners into the little town of Devil Pass. A shimmer of sunlight bounced off the roofs and sides of the buildings, painting the town red as he prodded his horse and prisoners down the street toward the sheriff's office. Next door to the sheriff's office was the Cattleman's Association and across the street from that was the Bottom Dollar Saloon. Sam was thirsty and he could almost taste the beer he would be drinking in a few minutes. His thirst was heightened by the large sign touting the saloon. It was a painting of a golden mug of beer, hanging out over the boardwalk, squeaking an invitation as it swung back and forth in the late-afternoon breeze.

Sam rode straight to the jail, then dismounted and signaled for his prisoners to do the same. Sheriff Butrum met them just in front of the door.

"Well, Sam, I see that you've brought me some business," he said. "Come on in, boys. I think you're going to like it here."

"You think you're going to keep us here, old man?" Quinn asked. "As soon as Pardeen finds out where we are, he's going to come in here and take this town apart. You just mark my words."

"Is that a fact?" Butrum replied. He opened the door. "Well, then, we'd better keep you where he can find you, don't you think? Come on inside, I have just the place for you."

Sam went in behind them, then walked over to the table alongside the wall and started leafing through the wanted posters. Butrum took the keyring down from a hook on the wall and opened one of the jail cells.

"Get in," Butrum said. It was more of an order than an invitation.

"I'm tellin' you, old man, you're makin' a very big mistake," Quinn said again.

"It won't be my first mistake," Butrum said. He slammed the door behind them, then turned the key in the lock.

"Maybe it ain't your first. But it could be your last," Zeke said ominously.

"Where'd you find them?" Butrum asked Sam as he walked over to rehang the key on the hook on the wall.

"About ten miles from here," Sam answered. "I found the place where they're all holed up, so, I just waited around outside long enough, and these two came out."

"Who are they, do you know?"

Sam took two posters from the pile and showed them to Butrum. "The tall one with the moustache is Zeke Tyler. The short one with the beard is L.Q. Quinn. They're small-fry, not more'n $100 on either one of them on their own. They wouldn't even be worth my time if the Association wasn't paying for them."

"I'll get word out to Doc Solinger that you brought two more in," Butrum said. "Where will I find you?"

"After I take care of the horses you'll find me in the saloon," Sam said. "Oh, and tell Solinger I brought both of them in alive, will you? He might appreciate that."

Butrum chuckled. "I'll give him the message."

Sam boarded his horse and the two horses belonging to the rustlers in the stable, then walked down to the Bottom Dollar Saloon. He saw that Fred was tending bar while Anne, the young bargirl he had "rescued" from Wiggins, was sitting at the back of the room near the piano. There were four cowhands sitting together at one of the tables and another customer standing at the bar, staring at the mug of beer in front of him.

Anne, recognizing Sam, smiled and walked over to stand beside him.

"Hi," she said. "Remember me?"

"The little girl with the black eye," Sam answered. "I hope you're being more careful about choosing your friends now."

"I'm trying to be," the girl said. She looked toward the bartender. "Give my friend a drink on me, Fred," she said.

Sam laughed at her. "Wait a minute. Don't you have that backwards?" he asked. "I thought the idea was for the customer to buy *you* a drink."

"Maybe it is," Anne said. "But right now, I figure I owe you."

"All right, if you insist. Thanks."

"What'll it be?" Fred asked.

"Beer."

Fred drew the beer, then put it on the bar. Sam blew some foam off the head, then drank the entire beer down before he lowered the mug. He set the empty stein on the bar and let out a long, satisfied sigh.

"That one was for thirst," he said. "Now I'll take one for taste."

"Be glad to," Fred replied, refilling his mug. When Sam started to pay, Fred waved him off. "No sir, Mr. Slater," he said. "Your money's no good in here."

"Your money's no good anywhere," Anne said, pointedly. "Out here or up there." With a lift of her eyes, she indicated the upstairs part of the saloon. "If you know what I mean."

Sam looked at her and raised the glass to his lips a second time. Anne was a young woman in her early twenties, with blond hair and blue eyes. Though some of the effects of her trade could be read in her eyes, dissipation had not yet taken its toll on her looks. She was still a very pretty girl.

"Yeah," Sam said. "Yeah, I guess I do know what you mean."

"Well, what do you say?"

Sam finished his second beer and set the empty down. "I say it would be downright rude not to accept your offer," he replied.

Anne smiled broadly. "This way," she invited, starting for the stairs that led to her room.

It was eleven o'clock that night and Sam was lying on the bed listening to the slow, steady breathing of the girl asleep beside him. He gave some consideration to staying the rest of the night with her but decided against it. Moving quietly so as not to waken her, not so much out of consideration for her sleeping habits as for the fact that he didn't want to answer questions as to why he was leaving, he got up, got dressed, then went downstairs. Waving at Fred, he walked through the bar and stepped out onto the front porch for some fresh air. That was when someone came running up to him, out of breath and clearly excited about something.

"Say, aren't you the bounty hunter that brought in them two rustlers today?"

"Yes."

"Iffen you don't want them to get away, you'd best get on down to the livery, right away," the man said.

"Why? What's happening?"

"While the sheriff was out makin' his rounds, them two prisoners somehow managed to get the jump on the boy that comes around ever' night to clean up the jail. The sheriff seen 'em just as they was gettin' away and he's got 'em holed up in the livery. The only thing is, they killed that clean-up boy so they say they ain't got nothin' to lose now, and they ain't goin' to give up. They say they're goin' to kill the livery boy if the sheriff don't let 'em go."

"Thanks," Sam said. He started down the street toward the livery and saw that there were a dozen or more people already gathered around the stable to watch the drama as it unfolded. He noticed, also, that none of them were offering to help the sheriff. He looked around for Butrum, but couldn't see him anywhere.

"Where's the sheriff?" he asked one of the men in the crowd.

"He's in there," the man said, pointing to the livery barn.

"Inside?"

"Yeah. He yelled out a moment ago that he was goin' to come in after them two if they didn't come out with their hands up. When they didn't come out, the sheriff went on inside."

"That seems like a dumb-fool thing to do," Sam said. Despite his comment, he couldn't help but have a begrudging respect for a man who, though already past his prime, was still willing to put his life on the line to do the job he was hired to do.

Sam pulled his own pistol and started toward the livery. He was almost there when he heard a muffled gunshot from the dark. He broke into a run and had just reached the edge of the stable when he saw Butrum coming out of the shadows toward him.

"Sheriff? Sheriff Butrum, what is it? What's going on?" Sam called. "I heard a shot."

"I'm killed, Sam," Butrum said with a half smile on his face. He fell, facedown to the ground, and Sam ran over to him and rolled him over.

"Sheriff?" Sam called, but there was no answer. Butrum was right, he had been killed.

"There goes one of 'em, Slater!" a man suddenly shouted from the other side of the livery. Sam drew his pistol and stared out into the empty darkness.

A figure suddenly appeared near the corner of the livery barn. He was tall and lanky and in the ambient light, Sam could see the walrus-type moustache. It was Zeke Tyler.

"Give it up, Zeke!" Sam called.

In answer, Zeke pointed his pistol toward Sam and it boomed three times. In the light of the muzzle flash, Sam could see the wild, desperate eyes.

Sam shot back only once, but once was enough. His bullet found its mark and Zeke threw up his gun and fell over backward. Sam ran over to the fallen outlaw and knelt beside him. He could see bubbles of blood coming from Zeke's mouth. Zeke was trying hard to breathe, and Sam heard a sucking sound in his chest. He knew that his bullet had punctured Zeke's lungs.

"Why didn't you give it up when I called to you?" Sam asked.

"I figure this beats hangin'," Zeke gasped.

"What about it, mister? Is he dead?" someone asked from behind Sam.

"He soon will be," Sam answered. He saw the townspeople beginning to stream across the street, drawn by morbid curiosity, anxious to get a look at the bodies of Sheriff Butrum and Zeke Tyler.

"Look at that," someone said, pointing to Zeke. "He got him dead center with one shot."

Frustrated by the gathering crowd, Sam stood up and waved at them. "Listen to me. You folks better get back if you don't want to get shot," he called. "There's still one left in the barn."

Almost as if in punctuation to Sam's statement, there was a flash of light, then the crash of gunfire as someone fired from inside the livery. Though the bullet didn't hit anyone, it whistled so close over the heads of the crowd that it had the effect that Sam's warning did not. With a shout of fear, everyone turned and ran to get out of the way of the line of fire.

"He's still in there!" someone said, repeating Sam's warning.

"The damn fool tried to shoot us," another said. The crowd, still unwilling to miss the show, stayed in close proximity. Now, however, they prudently found shelter behind the corners of adjacent buildings, or behind the nearby watering troughs.

"Quinn! Quinn, give it up," Sam called into the livery.

"Now why would I want to do that?" Quinn called back.

"Because you know I'm not goin' to let you come out of there alive, unless you *do* give yourself up."

"I ain't givin' up."

"Then you're going to die," Sam warned.

"I don't think so. I've got an edge, Slater."

"You've got nothing."

"I've got the stable man," Quinn called.

"So what?"

"So what? If you try and come in here, I'm goin' to kill him, that's so what."

"Go ahead. Kill him," Sam called back. He could hear the townspeople gasping around him.

"What? You're runnin' a bluff. You think I won't do it?"

"I don't care whether you do or not," Sam said. "You're worth $350 to me, dead or alive. That stable man isn't worth anything."

"You're . . . you're crazy. You know that?"

"Maybe," Sam said. "But I'm not the one trapped in a livery."

"Is Zeke dead?"

"Yes."

"It was him killed the sheriff. Not me," Quinn said. "All I wanted to do was get out of here."

"Is the stable man still alive?" Sam asked.

"Yes."

"Send him out."

"No. He's the only chance I have. If I come out, he's going to be standing in front of me."

"If he is, I'll kill him to get to you," Sam said.

"No, wait, wait!" Quinn called. "Maybe we can make a deal."

"What kind of deal?"

"I don't want to hang. I didn't kill the sheriff."

"Then let the stable man go. Maybe it'll make you look good for the jury."

"All right," Quinn called from the darkened interior. "All right, I'm comin' out now. I'm sending the stable man out first."

"Go ahead."

The door to the livery opened and the stable man stuck his head out, tentatively, then ran from the barn.

"He's out," Sam said. "Now it's your turn."

"Don't shoot."

"Come out with your hands up," Sam said. "I won't shoot."

Quinn, like the stable man before him, stuck his head around the edge of the door and searched anxiously up and down the street. He tossed his pistol out into the dirt.

"There," he called. "I ain't armed."

"Get your hands up and come on out."

Quinn stepped outside. Then, with his hands in the air, he started toward Sam. He took only three steps, when from one of the darkened buildings back in the town, a rifle barked. Quinn crumpled and went down.

"Who fired that shot?" Sam yelled over his shoulder. "Who fired?"

No one answered and Sam hurried over to Quinn's body.

"I thought you wouldn't shoot," Quinn coughed.

"I didn't," Sam answered. "I don't know who did it."

Quinn tried to laugh, but a spasm of coughing overtook him instead. "Why did he shoot me?" he asked. "I wasn't goin' to say anything."

"Why did who shoot you?"

Quinn's breath came in a series of raspy gasps.

"Quinn, who do you think shot you?"

The raspy gasps stopped and Sam put his hand to Quinn's neck. He was dead.

Once again the townspeople began to press forward. This time there was no one remaining to threaten their safety so that within a few moments the crowd around the three bodies had grown quite large.

"Well, Mr. Slater," Doc Solinger said. "I got word from Sheriff Butrum that you had brought in two live rustlers. Only by the time I got here, I learned that he was mistaken. Your prisoners are dead, and so is the sheriff."

"Yeah," Sam said.

"Death does seem to follow you, doesn't it?"

"I reckon it does."

Solinger sighed. "Well, there's no sense in belaboring the issue any longer. I have twice brought it to a vote to have you dismissed, and I have been defeated both times. If the Association wants to keep you on, to include your rather severe brand of justice, then I feel it is no longer my place to challenge you. Stop by tomorrow morning at seven o'clock. I'll have your money ready for you."

"Say, mister," the stable man said, coming up to Sam. "Would you really have killed me to get at him?" He nodded toward Quinn's body.

"Did you believe that?" Sam asked.

"You're damned right I believed it," the stable man replied.

"Then Quinn probably believed it, too," Sam said. "It took away his edge."

"But would you really have done it?"

Sam smiled. "If I told you, it would take away *my* edge," he said.

"Damn!" Pardeen said when he heard the news of what happened to Quinn and Zeke. "Slater again. I'm tellin' you, if we don't get rid of that son-of-a-bitch, he's going to get rid of us."

"Yeah, well, it ain't like we haven't been trying. He takes a lot of killin', that's all."

"Bullshit. He don't take no more killin' than anyone else," Pardeen said. "We just got to be a little smarter with it, that's all."

WHEN SAM DROPPED BY THE OFFICE OF the Cattleman's Association at seven the next morning, he learned that Doc Solinger had called a special meeting. Several of the ranchers' horses were already tied up at the hitching rail, a couple of buggies were parked on the street, and Vogel and Baker were just arriving.

"I heard about the little fracas last night," Baker said. "Congratulations on doin' a good job."

"Thanks," Sam said. He took in all the other horses with a sweep of his hand. "What's going on? Is there a meeting this morning?"

"Yes," Baker answered. "After Sheriff Butrum was killed last night, Doc Solinger sent word out to all of us, asking us to be here at seven this morning. You mean you don't know anything about it?"

"No," Sam answered. "I'm just here to collect my money. That is, unless this meeting is to suggest that I shouldn't be paid."

"Don't you worry none about that," Baker said. "Me and Vogel and Master and Hardin carry enough votes to see that that don't happen."

"Where is Hardin?" Vogel asked. "There's Master's horse, but I don't see Hardin's."

"I imagine he'll be along," Baker said and chuckled. "Until this meeting was called, there were several of us going to go over there and help him finish roofing his house, remember?"

"Yeah." Vogel laughed. "I don't reckon he'll want to tackle that job with just him and Shorty."

The other ranchers were already sitting around the meeting table when Sam, Baker, and Vogel went inside. Solinger was at the head of the table and with an expansive gesture, he invited them to sit down.

"Gentlemen, what do you say we get the meeting started?" Solinger began.

"Wait a minute. What about Hardin? He ain't here yet."

"Hardin won't be here, I'm afraid. He sent word that he wasn't going to be able to come. He has to run over to Sweetwater today." Solinger held up a piece of paper. "However, he gave me authorization to vote his proxy."

"Why'd he do that?" Baker asked.

"Why do you ask?"

"It's just that, you an' him don't always vote the same. Fact is, you been votin' contrary quite a bit here, lately. Seems strange to me that he'd give you his proxy, that's all."

"Don't worry about it. On any issue that I know he would disagree with me, I'll vote his proxy the way I think he would."

"That's all right by me," Masters said. "What about the rest of you?"

"I got no problems," Vogel said. "Baker?"

"I guess it's all right. But what's this meeting about, anyway?"

"A couple of things," Solinger said. He looked over at Sam. "To begin with, Mr. Slater, I've been pretty hard on you lately, and I want to apologize," he said. "Several of the good people of this town have told me what happened last night and, under the circumstances, there was nothing else you could do." He slid an envelope across the table toward him. "Your money is in this envelope and I want to go on record here and now as saying that you have my complete confidence. In fact, I would like to show that confidence by offering you the position of sheriff of Devil Pass. As you know, we are now in need of one."

"Thanks for the offer," Sam said, taking the envelope. "But I'm not interested in being a sheriff."

Solinger nodded. "That's all right, I didn't really think you would be. Nor should you be, actually. The truth is, you are much more effective the way you are. However, I thought it only right that the position be offered to you, before we offered it to anyone else." He looked at the others around the table. "However, gentlemen, his refusal does leave us with a problem. We have to have a new sheriff and I'm asking for any suggestions."

"What about you, Doc?" one of the other ranchers proposed.

"Me? No, I don't see myself as sheriff."

"Wait a minute, why not?" Masters asked. "You're the head of the Cattleman's Association. You could combine the two jobs."

"Gentlemen, you forget, I have a ranch to run. A larger ranch, I might add, than any of you."

"Well, yes, but you've found the time to be

president of the Cattleman's Association. You can find time to do this as well. It needs doin', Doc, you can't get around that."

"But being a sheriff is a full-time job."

"It don't have to be. I mean, you've got a foreman to help with the ranch, and you can appoint as many deputies as you want to help with the sheriffing," one of the other men said. "Come on, Doc, we're not sayin' you have to make night rounds like Butrum did. Just sort of be over things."

"Like a general," another suggested.

"A general," Solinger said. He smiled. "I like that." He drummed his fingers on the table for a while, then he nodded his head. "All right," he said. "I am committed to running the rustlers out and bringing peace to the valley. And if the only way to do that is to be your sheriff, then I'll be your sheriff. But only until this business is all taken care of. After that, like a general after a war is over, I intend to go back being a private citizen and a rancher. A prosperous rancher, I hope."

The others laughed, then there was a spattering of applause around the table. Solinger looked over at Sam.

"Mr. Slater, now that I am officially the sheriff I'll say the same thing I said a few moments ago as a rancher and as the head of the

Cattleman's Association. I appreciate, that is, we all appreciate the job you've been doing and you have my full and complete support."

"Thanks," Sam said again. He stood up. "Now, if you men will excuse me, I'm going to get a little breakfast, then go back to work."

"Good luck to you," Solinger said. "Now, gentlemen, I want to talk about the price per head at the cattle pens in Kansas City. I think we can . . ." That was as far as Solinger got before Sam left the office and walked across the street to the Alhambra Cafe.

Sam ate so many of his meals out on the range that when he did have the chance to eat in town, he ate well. Breakfast this morning consisted of a stack of pancakes, two eggs, fried potatoes, an over-sized piece of ham, and half-a-dozen biscuits. He was just washing it all down with a second cup of coffee when an old, Mexican woman came into the cafe, looked around until she saw him, then shuffled over to his table.

"You are Senor Slater?" she asked.

"Yes."

"This is for you." She handed him a note.

SLATER,

WE HAVE THE HARDIN GIRL.

PARDEEN

"Wait!" Sam called, standing up quickly. The woman stopped. "Where did you get this?"

"A man gave it to me," she answered. "He gave me money to give it to you."

"What man?"

"I do not know him, senor. I do laundry at the edge of town. He rode in on a horse, gave me the note, then rode away."

"Thanks," Sam said. He looked at the note for a moment, then, with a sigh of frustration, put it in his pocket.

He was now faced with the very situation he always tried to avoid. Because of the kind of life he led, he made it a practice never to establish relationships with anyone, male or female. This wasn't because of any particular antisocial behavior on his part, this was based upon a very sound principle. Sam knew he could always be responsible for himself, but he couldn't always be responsible for anyone else. That wasn't a very healthy situation, for if he was close to anyone, an enemy could get to him through that person. On the other hand, if he was close to no one, an enemy would have no way to get to him. In this way, he denied any potential enemy an "edge."

For the most part, Sam's theory worked well. Sometimes, however, there were those borderline cases where he was vulnerable, and

Cindy Hardin was just such a case. Though no official relationship had been established between the two of them, their paths had crossed frequently enough that he could no longer regard her with total detachment. He had come to her rescue once on the train, and again when the outlaws had raided the Hardin ranch. Even the horse he was riding now had been a gift from Cindy Hardin and her father. If Pardeen did have her, Sam knew he had no choice. He would have to go after her.

Pardeen had found his edge. Sam didn't like it much when the other fellow had an edge.

At first it was just a thin wisp, looking like nothing more than a column of dust in the distance. But as he drew closer to the Hardin ranch the wisp of dust took on more substance until it became a column of smoke, growing thicker and heavier as he approached, until finally it was a heavy, black cloud filled with glowing embers and rolling into the sky.

This was Pardeen's second visit to the ranch, and as before, he had left fire and smoke as his calling cards. Once again, Pardeen was burning them out.

The fire was still snapping and popping when Sam arrived but there was little left to burn. The new house, so recently built to replace the one that had been burned out before, was now a twisted mass of blackened timbers with just enough fuel left to support the dying flames.

Pardeen had been more thorough this time than he had been before, because this time the barn, bunkhouse, and grainery were also in flames. In addition to the fires there had been a wanton slaughter of all the farm animals. Two dray-horses lay dead in the corral, half-a-dozen pigs were slaughtered, and there were even a handful of dead chickens scattered about.

Sam saw Hardin then, facedown in a pool of his own blood. When he went over to get a closer look at the rancher, he saw that the older man had been shot several times in the head and chest. He knew, even before he reached im, that Hardin was dead. Martha, also dead, was lying nearby, at his side in death as she had been in life.

"Slater? Slater, is that you?" The voice that called was strained with pain and when Sam looked toward it, he saw Shorty on the ground over near the watering trough. He hurried over to him. "We sure could've used your gun this time, partner," Shorty said.

"When did this happen?" Sam asked.

"This mornin', just after daylight," Shorty

answered. "We sure wasn't expectin' nothin' like this. They wasn't after to steal nothin'. They just come out here to murder and to burn. They went plumb crazy. After they shot me an' Mr. and Mrs. Hardin, they commenced to killin' all the animals. No reason for it, they didn't take no meat nor nothin', they just killed and killed and killed. By then there wasn't nothin' left I could do, so I just lay over here real still and pretended to be dead." He sat up and Sam saw that he had at least three bullet holes in him, two in the thigh and one in the arm. They were painful and he had lost a lot of blood, but he would probably live.

"Who did this, Shorty? Was it Pardeen?"

"Yeah, it was Pardeen. Him and about eight others," Shorty said. "I got two of 'em. You'll find 'em over there, both dead. But there's six of 'em left."

"You did all you could do," Sam said.

Suddenly Shorty reached up and grabbed Sam's arm and squeezed it tight, as if just remembering something that was important. "They got Cindy, Slater. They got Cindy and they took her off with them. She was callin' for me to help her but I . . . I couldn't do nothin' for her. Go after her, Slater. Get her back from those bastards."

"They're using her as bait," Sam said. "They took her to get me to come after them."

"Are you goin' after her?"

"I don't know," Sam said. "I do know that that's what they want me to do."

Shorty raised his gun and pointed it at Sam, though he had such little strength to keep it up that the barrel weaved around in tiny circles.

"Damnit, man," Shorty said. "Didn't you hear what I said? They got Cindy! Now, tell me you're going to bring her back safe, or so help me God, I'll shoot you myself."

"Don't worry, I'm going after her," Sam said easily. "I'll bring her back, I promise."

"I'm goin' to hold you to that, Slater," Shorty said. "I can't go myself, so you're the only chance she's got."

"I'll get her," Sam promised, hating the fact that he had let himself get so involved, yet determined to follow through with his promise.

"Thanks," Shorty said. He smiled broadly. "I knew you'd go after her," he said. He lowered the gun, then smiled. "Couldn't have shot you anyway," he said. "I already used up all the bullets. That's why I had to just lie here an' watch helplessly."

"Which way did they go, Shorty?"

"North."

"North?" That surprised Sam. He had located their hideout and it was south of the ranch. However, they may know by now that he had found them. If so, they would have to go someplace else.

"Slater. Cindy's wearin' a red dress. You ought to be able to spot that a mile away."

"Thanks."

"Bring her back to me, Slater. There's something' I ain't ever got aroun' to tellin' her yet."

Cindy sat on her horse looking at Pardeen and the others who had come to kill her ma and pa and Shorty, then burn her ranch. Pardeen was holding his hat in his hand, wiping his hairless brow with a bandanna. He looked back at Cindy and laughed, a greasy, evil-sounding laugh.

"How are you doin' little lady? Are you holdin' up all right?"

"I find it hard to believe that you are actually concerned about my comfort," Cindy replied sarcastically.

"Yeah, sure," Pardeen said. "After all, I want to be a good host." He laughed at his own joke.

"Why did you kill all the others but take me?"

"Why do you care? You're alive, ain't you? Ain't that all that's important?"

"No. There are some things that are more important than merely being alive."

"Yeah? Well, maybe for folks like you, folks who are noble and all that. But I ain't noble. Tell me about Slater."

"What?" Cindy asked, surprised by the question.

"Sam Slater, the fella they call The Regulator. Tell me about him."

"What do you want to know? He's a good man."

"Will he come for you?"

"Will he come for me? I don't know. Why should he come for me?"

"Because I sent him a note tellin' him I had you," Pardeen said.

"Why would you do that?"

"Don't you understand anything at all? I'm usin' you, girlie. I'm usin' you as bait."

Pardeen pulled his pistol and turned the cylinder to check the loads, then put the pistol back in his holster.

"You did all this, just to get Sam Slater to come after you?" Cindy asked. "You're mad!

He's been after you all along. That's the whole reason he is here."

"Yeah, well, I want him on my own terms," Pardeen said. "From what I hear, he's not the kind of man you mess with. They say he was fast when he gunned down Murdock. As fast as greased lightnin'." Pardeen pulled his lips tight across his teeth in what might have been a smile. "I'm pretty fast, too. When he comes for you, me an' him's goin' to have a little face-to-face meetin'."

"If he's as fast as you think, why would you want to face him? Aren't you afraid he might kill you?"

"I figure on tippin' the odds in my favor a bit," Pardeen said. "After I kill him, I'll be known all over as the man who got Slater. That'd be a good reputation for a man of my profession to carry 'round with him."

"Profession? What kind of profession do you have besides murder and robbery?" Cindy asked sharply.

"I'm a professional shootist," Pardeen said proudly. "Them other things, the murder and robbery, why, they just sort of go with the territory, that's all."

While Pardeen talked, Cindy was working on a part of her dress, rubbing it against a rough corner on her saddle pommel. Now, at last, she had the dress shredded so she could tear off little pieces one at a time. She dropped a piece on the ground then looked down to see the little bit of red cloth.

Please, dear God, she prayed silently. *Let Sam Slater find this trail I'm leaving for him.*

AHEAD OF SAM, THE BROWN LAND LAY IN empty folds of rocks, dirt, and cactus. The sun heated the ground, then sent up undulating waves that caused nearby objects to shimmer and nonexistent lakes to appear tantalizingly in the distance. Sam picked up the tracks of seven riders, but the ground was hard and the tracks so indistinct that he couldn't tell very much about them. He didn't know if Cindy was one of the riders or not. Then, he saw a piece of red cloth hanging in one of the mesquite bushes and knew that Cindy was with them, and that he was on the right track. It also told him that she was all right.

"Good girl, Cindy," he said as he pulled the cloth off the branch and stuck it in his pocket.

About an hour after he found the first bit of cloth, he found another. This time it not only told him he was still on the right trail, it saved his life. That was because the second piece of red cloth was lying on the ground and he got off his horse to pick it up. Just as he was dismounting, a pistol boomed and the ball sizzled by, taking his hat off and fluffing his hair. Had he maintained his seat, he would be dead now.

Moving quickly, Sam slapped his horse's flank to get him out of the line of fire, then dove for a nearby rock just as a second shot whizzed by. He wriggled his body under cover, then raised himself slowly to take a look around. He saw the crown of a hat poking over the top of a rock so he aimed and shot. The hat went sailing away.

"You just put a hole in a twenty-dollar hat, you son-of-a-bitch!" the ambusher called.

"Yeah? I meant to put one in your head."

The ambusher fired again and this bullet was as close as the first one. It hit the rock right in front of Sam and kicked tiny pieces of rock and shreds of hot lead into his face before it whined away from him. Sam turned around and slid down to the ground, brushing the hot lead from his cheeks.

The ambusher laughed. "Pretty close, wasn't I? Did that sting a little?"

"Where's the girl?" Sam called.

"The girl? She's with Pardeen and the others," the voice answered.

"They leave you behind for the dirty work?"

"No. I volunteered to stay behind. You see, we've got us a pretty good pot built up for whoever kills you. I reckon that's goin' to be me."

"I doubt it. You've already missed your chance."

"They say you're pretty fast," the ambusher called. "How fast?"

"Fast enough to stay alive."

"Well, I don't think fast counts, Mr. Regulator. I think the only thing that counts is a measure of guts. And I got that. The name's Mayhan. Eddie Mayhan. You ever heard of me?"

"I've seen paper on you," Sam admitted. "You're not worth much. About $150, I think."

"Yeah? Well, after I kill you, I reckon I'll be worth more," Mayhan said.

"You aren't afraid of me, Mayhan?"

"Naw, I ain't afraid. The way I've heard it,

you do most of your shootin' in the back, or against blowhards like Murdock. He *was* a blowhard, you know."

"I'd say you called it about right," Sam replied. "Murdock was pretty much of a blowhard." He moved around, trying to get into position to see his assailant.

"Say, Slater, how'd you like it if we was to both put our guns in our holsters then step out into the open, just to see how things would come out?"

"What?" Sam asked, surprised by the challenge. "Let me get this straight, you're offering to go up against me?"

"Yeah. I told you, I ain't like the others. I ain't all that fast but I don't figure you have to be. And I sure ain't goin' to pee in my pants just 'cause you say boo. I believe I can take you. What do you say you put your gun away and step out to try me?"

Sam looked around the rock and saw that the other man was coming from behind his cover with his pistol holstered and his hands spread out beside him.

"Come on, Mr. Regulator. I'm already out here."

Sam holstered his own pistol, then stood up.

"Well, I'll be damned," Sam said. "I didn't really think you'd do it."

"Well, I'm a surprising man," Mayhan said, grinning evilly. "Now!" he suddenly shouted.

A pistol shot went off from Sam's immediate right. The bullet missed, though Sam didn't know how it could have, because he was so close to the hidden assailant that he felt the sting of burnt gunpowder.

"Arnie, you dumb bastard! You missed!" Mayhan shouted as he went for his own gun.

Sam had a fifth of a second to make a decision. Should he fire at Eddie Mayhan who was just now going for his gun, or should he shoot at Arnie, who was now rising up from behind a nearby rock with his gun already in his hand? Sam decided to take on Mayhan. Arnie had already demonstrated his poor marksmanship in the missed shot, whereas Mayhan had come much closer on his first shot.

Even as he was thinking about it, Sam's gun was cocked and booming. The bullet slammed into Mayhan's chest, severing arteries and tearing away heart tissue. Mayhan was dead before he hit the ground, and even before he fell, Sam was already turning to fire at Arnie. Arnie's second shot proved as ineffective as his first, but Sam's bullet hit Arnie in the hip, causing him to double over, then crumple down in pain.

Sam stood quietly for a moment as the echoes of the shots came rolling back from a nearby rock wall. When the last echo was a subdued rumble off a distant hill, the silence of the desert returned. The limbs of a nearby ocotillo rattled dryly in the breeze. A shock of tumbleweed bounced by. A lizard scurried across a rock.

"Oh," Arnie moaned. "Oh, shit, it hurts. I ain't never had nothin' to hurt like this."

"Where is Pardeen?" Sam asked. "And the Hardin girl? Where are they?"

"I'm gutshot," Arnie said.

Sam looked at the bullet hole. It was in the hip, painful but not fatal.

"You aren't gutshot."

"I'm goin' to die."

"No, you won't. Not unless I kill you. Where are Pardeen and the girl?"

"I can't tell you that. Pardeen will kill me if I tell you."

"I'll kill you if you don't."

Arnie shook his head no.

"If that's the way you want it," Sam said easily. He pointed his pistol at Arnie's head and cocked it. The cylinder turned with a metallic click, lining up the next cartridge under the hammer and firing pin. The knuckle of his trigger finger whitened.

"No!" Arnie screamed, covering his head with his arms. "No, don't kill me!"

"Where's the girl?" Sam asked again.

"This ambush wasn't my idea," Arnie said. "It was Pardeen's. He told us he'd double the pot if me and Mayhan would stay back and take care of you."

"One last time. Where is the girl?"

"All I know is they were headed for a little Mex town called Mezquita."

"Give me your gun," Sam said.

"What?"

"I said, give me your gun."

"Look here, Slater. You ain't goin' to leave me out here unarmed, are you? There might be Indians around. Snakes, wolves, all sorts of things."

"I'm doin' you a favor," Sam said. "The way you shoot, you're likely to shoot yourself."

Sam took Arnie's pistol, then he took the pistol from Mayhan's hand.

"Where are your horses?"

"Right over there, behind them rocks," Arnie answered, pointing off to his left.

Keeping Arnie covered, Sam walked over and retrieved the two horses. He shoved the pistols into the saddle bag of one of the animals.

"Take off your boots," Sam ordered.

Arnie did as he was instructed and Sam put the boots in the stirrups, then slapped the horses on the flanks, sending them running.

"Wait a minute! You're leavin' me out here with no horse, no water, and no boots," Arnie complained. "You can't do that! I'll die!"

"There's a town about six miles that way," Sam said, pointing to the southeast. "You can make it there. Try to go anywhere else and you *will* die. You better get goin' now. The longer you stay out here, the thirstier you're goin' to get."

"I'll get you for this, Slater," Arnie said, shaking his fist at Sam. "One of these days we'll run across each other again and when we do, I'll get you."

"Yeah, keep thinking about that," Sam suggested. "It'll keep you going."

Arnie started toward the southeast, his progress impeded not only by his lack of boots, but also by the fact that he was carrying a bullet in his hip. Sam watched for a moment, then swung into the saddle and rode north, heading toward Mezquita.

* * *

Mezquita was no different from any of the other Mexican towns scattered throughout the American Southwest. The Mexican flavor dictated its layout—a dozen or more adobe buildings scattered around a large square. This village did happen to have a church, though, a large mission which stood guard at the south end of town. The shadow of the cross fell across Sam's face as he rode into the churchyard. The padre was drawing water from a well and Sam got down and walked toward him. The priest wore a brown cassock, held together with a strip of black rawhide, from which dangled an oversized, wooden crucifix. A bald spot shone from the top of the priest's head. The hair around the bald spot was gray.

"Padre," Sam said, nodding at the priest.

The priest nodded back, studying Sam closely.

"I'd be obliged for a drink," Sam said. "The water in my canteen has grown a little stale." He pulled out a couple of bills and handed them to the priest.

"This is God's water," the priest said, waving the money away. "It's free."

"The money isn't for His water, it's for His church," Sam said.

The priest smiled. "*Sí, gracias*. Bless you, my son, bless you," he said, taking the money.

Sam plunged the dipper into the bucket and scooped up the water, then drank long and deep. It was cool and delicious, and he drank until his belly was full. Then he wiped his mouth with the back of his hand.

"Would you like to fill your canteen?" the priest offered.

"Yes, thank you," Sam said. He lifted the canteen from his saddle, poured out the old water, then began refilling it with fresh water from the dipper. "Padre, I'm looking for some men who may have come in here. There would be four of them. Four men, and one girl. The girl with them would be young and pretty. Also, she would be wearing a red dress.

"These men," the priest asked. "Are they friends of yours?"

"No, I wouldn't call them friends."

"I did not think so," the priest replied. The priest looked at Sam for a long moment. Sam felt strange, as if the priest's eyes could penetrate to his very soul. Under the priest's gaze he was stripped naked with all his past sins, actual and conceived, bared. "I am confused," the priest finally said.

"What has you confused?"

"You have come to kill these men. This I know, for there is death in your eyes. You are a man who has killed many times, but I do not see pleasure in the killing."

"Padre, the men I seek are very evil," Sam said. "They have killed many times, and they *do* kill for pleasure. They killed the girl's mother and father, and all those who worked on the girl's ranch."

"If I tell you and you kill them, I will be a party to it," the priest said. "I do not wish to help you kill the men."

"I think when they are through with the girl, they will kill her. If you do not wish to help me kill the men, then consider that you are helping me save the girl."

"Sí. Sí, I will help the girl," the padre said. "Very well, the men you are seeking, four men and a girl, rode into town early today. Then, a bit later, three men and the girl rode out."

"Only three rode out? Then that means one of the men is still here."

"Sí."

"What does he look like?"

"This I cannot tell you," the priest said. "I did not see any of them closely."

"Thank you," Sam said. "You have been a big help."

"I will pray for the safety of the girl, senor," the priest said.

* * *

The entrance into the cantina was protected, not by bat-wing doors as was routine in the more Americanized towns, but by several strings of beads. Sam stood on the porch just outside the cantina for a long moment, listening to the sounds from inside. Someone was strumming a guitar but that didn't stop the flow of conversation. The words were Mexican mostly, though he heard a few English-speaking voices. The beads clacked against each other as Sam pushed through to step inside.

Pulling his hat brim low, he stepped up to the end of the bar, then looked through the place. There were more than three dozen men and women inside. Several were standing at the bar, many others were sitting around the tables. One Mexican was in a chair against the wall holding a pretty girl, obviously one of the bargirls, on his lap.

It appeared that there were only four Americans. Sam figured that his man had to be one of them, so he studied them closely. But then of course, the cantina did have a few rooms in the back to be used by the whores. It was possible that his man could be back there. He slapped the bar.

"Sí?" the bartender asked, sliding down the bar to stand before him.

"Beer."

"We have only tequila."

"All right," Sam said, putting his coin on the bar.

The bartender filled a glass and Sam took a drink, screwing his face up against its controlled fire.

One of the Americans laughed. "What's the matter, mister? You don't like Mexican mule piss?" he asked. The others laughed with him.

"Sure," Sam answered. "I like it just fine."

"Say, why don't you come over here and join us in a friendly game of cards?" one of the other cowboys called. "We don't get too many Americans through here."

"Yeah," the first one said. "There's just the four of us and we get tired of looking at each other's ugly mugs every day."

Sam took his drink over to the table and sat down to join them. "You mean all four of you live here?

"Yeah. I'm Slim, that's Beans, he's Poke and that's Dusty. We cowboy for Senor Soltano. Ain't that somethin' though? I mean a bunch of Americans workin' for a Mexican."

"Soltano is Mex, all right, but he's fair and he pays good wages," Beans said.

"Yeah," Slim agreed. "He's a good man. Don't get us wrong, we ain't apologizin' for workin' for him or nothin'. Just remarkin' on it, that's all."

Sam studied the men closely and realized that they were telling the truth. They had the look of cowboys, in their faces and in their eyes. Also, their hands were callused from hard work. These weren't outlaws.

"Are there rooms back there?" Sam asked, pointing toward the rear of the building.

"Yeah," Slim answered, laughing. "You wantin' to go back there?"

"If you do, ask ole' Dusty here which one of these girls is best. He knows 'em all," Poke teased and the others laughed at Dusty's expense.

"Anyone back there now?" Sam asked. "Americans, I mean?"

"Ain't no other Americans here a'tall 'cept just what's sittin' around this table," Slim said.

"Why do you ask?" Poke inquired.

"No reason in particular," Sam answered. "I stopped down at the church to fill my canteen and the padre said four American men and one girl rode in today. I was just curious about them, that's all."

"Yeah, well, a group of them rode in today, but they didn't stay."

"No, they come in and bought a bottle then went right on. Weren't very friendly."

"Anyhow, they wasn't all Americans," Slim said.

"What?"

"They wasn't all Americans," Slim insisted. "Three of them was, and I think the girl was, but she stayed outside on her horse and didn't come in so I never got a good look at her. She didn't say nothing' a'tall."

"What color dress was she wearing?"

"It was red," Poke said. "You fellas remember that 'cause Dusty said they weren't nothin' no prettier than a woman in a red dress."

"I thought you didn't get a good look at her," Sam said.

Slim laughed. "Dusty don't have to get a good look. To him all women is pretty, whether they be wearin' a red dress or not."

"The other man was Mex," Dusty said.

"What?"

"The fourth man," Dusty said. "He was Mex."

"Yeah, come to think of it, he was," Slim agreed. "And he didn't ride out with the others, neither. I don't remember seein' him leave."

Sam had no idea what made him look around at that precise moment. Maybe it was the fact that he had just learned that one of the men he was looking for was Mexican, and he decided to look again at those in the bar. Or maybe he heard something. Or, maybe it was true what they sometimes said of gunfighters, that they had a sixth sense about danger. For whatever reason, Sam looked around, just as the Mexican against the wall was dumping the bar girl from his lap. She screamed in surprise and fright as the Mexican came up with a pistol in his hand.

"What the hell?" Slim asked. "You fellas look out!" He and the other cowboys dove for the floor just as the Mexican fired.

Sam brought his own gun up, even as the Mexican's gun burst the firing-cap. The Mexican's bullet hit the deck of cards the cowboys had been playing with, sending them scattering. The cowboys weren't the only ones on the floor. By now everyone else in the place had also dove for cover, leaving only Sam and the Mexican standing. But the Mexican didn't stand for long because Sam fired before the Mexican could pull the trigger a second time.

The heavy slug from Sam's gun sent the Mexican crashing through a nearby table. Glasses and bottles tumbled and tequila spilled to merge with the blood which was already beginning to pool on the floor. The gunsmoke drifted slowly up to the ceiling, then spread out in a wide, nostril-burning cloud. Sam looked around the room quickly to see if anyone else might represent danger, but he saw only the faces of the customers and they showed only fear, awe, and surprise.

"Damn!" Dusty said into the silence that followed the two gunshots.

"Was he the one with the Americans?" Sam asked.

Poke repeated the question in Spanish, and half-a-dozen of the Mexican customers nodded in the affirmative.

"Yeah, he was," Poke said.

"Is he dead?"

Again the question was repeated in Spanish, and one of those who had hurried over to look at him nodded yes. "Sí, senor. He is dead."

"Damn. I didn't want to kill him," Sam said. "I needed some information from him."

"You didn't want to kill him, huh?" Slim asked. He chuckled. "Well, you shot pretty straight for someone who didn't want him dead."

IT WAS VERY LATE IN THE AFTERNOON BEfore Sam saw another little piece of cloth about a mile north of Mezquita. It had been quite a while since she had left any sort of a trail marker and he realized she was probably being watched pretty closely. Very near the marker he also saw some horse-droppings and could tell that he was gaining on them.

It was another thirty minutes before he was shot at from ambush. He didn't hear or suspect anything until the moment the bullet hit him. A sudden, numbing, sledge-hammer blow to his arm knocked him from his horse.

Immediately after that, a man jumped out from behind a rock and charged after him, firing his pistol as he ran. The bullets hit the ground around him, ricocheted off the rocks, then sailed off, filling the canyon with their angry whine.

Sam was hit in his left arm and that caused him to fall on his right side. He was lying on his right side, the gun side, and thus was unable to get to his pistol. Finally he managed to force himself over onto his left side, banging his wounded arm painfully against the rocks while he grabbed for his gun. By the time he managed to get it out of his holster, his assailant had closed to within three feet.

"I've got you, Slater! I've got you!" the man yelled, excitedly, pointing his pistol at Sam's head.

Sam didn't have time to aim his gun. Instead he turned it up from his waist and pulled the trigger, shooting by feel. His bullet tore into his attacker's throat. The man gagged, dropped his gun, and put both hands to his neck. Sam shot again and this time his bullet hit the man right in the middle of the face, tearing away his nose.

As the man dropped, Sam, knowing now how they operated, stood up and looked around for a second ambusher. He heard a horse riding away and climbed quickly up a nearby rock formation to try and get another shot. He was too late, however. Whoever it was got away.

Cindy and her captors had reached an old, deserted line cabin earlier that afternoon. Now Cindy lay on an old cot, her hands tied to what was left of the headboard and her feet tied at the broken footrail. During the long afternoon, she had watched the dust-laden sunbeams as they criss-crossed throughout the darkened interior of the cabin, forming little spears of light to stab through the cracks in the walls and gaps and holes in the shake-shingled roof. Now the bright spears of light were gone, to be replaced by the dim glow of early evening.

Eight outlaws had come to burn the ranch and kill her ma, pa, and Shorty. She had watched from the house and saw Shorty kill two of the outlaws before he went down himself. Then, when it was over, the six outlaws who were left took her prisoner.

When they left the burning ranch, there had been seven, counting her: Pardeen, four other Americans and a Mexican. But two of the Americans and the Mexican dropped off during the long ride and didn't return. Pardeen was agitated by that. Cindy knew this, because she overheard a conversation between Pardeen and the other two men this afternoon, just before the other two men rode off.

"He couldn't have killed all three of them," Pardeen told the men. "The bastards must've run out on us."

"They wouldn't run out on us, Pardeen. Hell, I know Eddie wouldn't," one of the men said. This was the one Cindy had heard referred to as Boone. "I'm tellin' you, somethin' must've happened to him. Whyn't you let me and Smitty go back and wait on him? We'll pick us out some place and kill the son-of-a-bitch from ambush."

"All right, Boone, you two go ahead," Pardeen agreed. "I'll wait for you here. But as soon as the bastard is dead you come back here and tell me, you hear? You come back here and tell me."

"We'll come back," Boone promised.

That had been over two hours ago and they weren't back yet. As a result, Pardeen was pacing back and forth in the little cabin, going over to the window every couple of minutes to look outside.

"They aren't coming back," Cindy said.

"You," Pardeen said, turning away from

the window and pointing at her, "just keep your mouth shut."

"I was just telling you what you already know," she said.

"I mean it," Pardeen said again. "Just keep your mouth shut or I'll gag you."

Cindy shut up, but she continued to watch Pardeen's every move, riveting him with her eyes. He broke out into a heavy sweat and kept wiping his face and the top of his head.

"Quiet!" he said a moment later, though she hadn't made a sound. "I hear someone." He drew his pistol and stood at the window, staring through it. Suddenly he turned around with a big grin on his face. "It's Smitty," he said. "He's back. I guess you know what that means. Slater's dead." He walked over and looked down at the cot. "Not much point in keepin' you around any longer now, is there?" he asked.

Cindy heard the horse stop out front, then the door opened and Smitty came bounding in.

"The son-of-a-bitch killed Boone," Smitty said.

"What? I thought you were going to shoot him from ambush."

"Hell, we did," Smitty said. "I hit him and knocked him down off his horse. Then Boone, I don't know, he just went sort of crazy. Maybe it was because he thought I was goin' to get the credit or somethin'. Anyway, he just run out at Slater, shootin' wild, an' Slater killed 'im."

"But you said you got him. You said you knocked him off his horse."

"Hell, I did. But I must've just winged him or somethin', 'cause the son-of-a-bitch was able to shoot Boone and now he's comin' after us."

"All right. All right, then we'll just be waitin' for him."

"*You* wait for him," Smitty said. "I ain't stayin' aroun' here. No, sir. There ain't no way I'm goin' to go up against Slater again."

"You ain't runnin' out on me?" Pardeen asked.

"The hell I ain't. And if you got 'ny sense, you will, too. Come on, leave the girl an' let's go."

"We're staying," Pardeen insisted.

"I'm not," Smitty said. "I wouldn't even stopped by here 'ceptin' to warn you." Smitty started for the door but before he reached it, there was a gunshot, then a billow of smoke filled the cabin. Smitty spun around with a surprised look on his face and saw Pardeen standing there, holding the smoking gun in his hand. Smitty put his hand around to his back, trying to find the bullet hole, but he couldn't reach it. "You shot me!" he said.

Smitty pitched forward onto his face. He tried to get back up, raised up to his hands and knees, then went down again. This time he lay still and after a couple of gasping breaths, he was dead.

"I told you," Pardeen said under his breath. "You wasn't leavin'."

The night air felt refreshingly cool after the long, hot day. Sam dismounted, left his horse hobbled about one hundred yards away from the little cabin, then approached it on foot. He slipped through the shadows until he was just outside the cabin, then edged along the wall until he could look through a gap between the boards. Incredibly, there was a candle burning inside, thus allowing him to see what was going on.

Sam saw Cindy staked out on the bunk, and two men in the front of the cabin, looking out through the two front windows. Pardeen was very animated, moving back and forth nervously, while the other man was absolutely still. There was something strange about the second person, but Sam didn't know what it was.

The problem, as Sam saw it, was that

there was only one way into the cabin, and that was through the front door. And Pardeen had the front door so well covered that there was no way he could get in without affording the outlaw a clear line of fire.

The cabin was old and had probably been abandoned for a long time. That explained all the gaps in the wall, the collapsed porch, and the caved-in roof.

There were no windows at the back of the cabin, so Sam went around behind, found the exposed beam of a rafter and used it to pull himself up onto the roof. Lying on his stomach he moved across top of the cabin, slowly, quietly, testing the shingles until he could find several that were loose and rotten. He pulled one aside, then looked through. Pardeen was still pacing around nervously, but the other man had not moved since the first time Sam saw him.

"Where is he?" Sam heard Pardeen ask. "Why don't he come?"

"He's waiting for you to make a mistake," Cindy said.

"Shut up!" Pardeen replied, whirling around toward her. He pointed his gun at her. "The only thing keepin' you alive now is I might need you. But if you don't keep that mouth of yours shut, I'll shoot you whether I need you or not."

Sam realized that Pardeen was getting very nervous, and the more nervous he got, the more dangerous it would be for Cindy. He had to do something and he had to do it soon.

Sam studied the roof for a moment, then saw that there was one area that was covered by four or five rotten shingles. He could break them off easily, but if he did, Pardeen would surely hear him the moment he started.

Then he got an idea. He wouldn't break them off one at a time, he would break them off all at once. But the only way he could do that would be to jump right through them. And that meant a drop of eight to ten feet to the floor below.

Sam stood up quietly, took a deep breath, then leaped right into the middle of the rotten shingles and crashed through the roof.

Cindy was as shocked as Pardeen when she saw Sam suddenly burst through the roof and fall to the floor. She let out a little scream of surprise.

"What the hell!" Pardeen shouted, swinging around from the window to blaze away at the intruder. A long finger of flame spit from the end of his gun and the heavy slug tore into the floor where landed. It would have hit Sam, had he not rolled to his left the moment he fell. Sam fired as he rolled, and Pardeen went down, clawing at a hole next to his heart. Sam rolled again and turned his gun toward the second man, who still hadn't turned around.

"He's dead!" Cindy explained.

Sam raised his gun up.

"Pardeen shot him when he thought he was going to run away," Cindy went on. "He stuck him up in the window to fool you into thinking there were two of them in here."

Sam chuckled. "It worked," he said. "I was fooled." He put his gun away then, and went over to the cot to untie the ropes that held Cindy bound. "Are you all right?"

"Yes," Cindy said. As soon as she was untied, she ringed Sam's neck with her arms and hugged him, hard. "Thank you," she said. "I knew you would come."

"It's all over now," Sam said, gently. "Come on, I'll take you back home."

"Home?" Cindy said. Tears came to her eyes. "What's there to go home to? Ma and Pa are both dead. So's Shorty. And the ranch is burned."

"The buildings are burned," Sam said. "But the land is still there. So are the cattle." He smiled. "And so is Shorty."

"What?" Cindy gasped. "But I saw him . . ."

"You saw him shot," Sam interrupted. "But he didn't die and he's not going to."

"Thank God," Cindy said, crying with relief.

Sam looked over at the two bodies. "That one is worth too much money to leave here," he said, pointing to Pardeen. "So I'm going to pack him back with us. I'll bury the other man. Why don't you get a little rest. It's too late to start back now; we'll leave at first light."

About three miles away from the cabin, Evan McAlister came across Boone's body. He chuckled.

"Oh, you're good, Slater. You're damn good," he said. "Maybe even the best around, next to me," he added. He stood up and walked over to his horse and patted the polished stock of the Whitworth. "By this time tomorrow, you'll be belly-down across your horse and I'll be $9,000 richer."

McAlister had already heard the story, how Pardeen had burned out the Hardin ranch, killed the girl's parents, and stolen the girl. Sam had gone after her.

There were some back in Devil Pass who figured Slater had bitten off more than he could chew. There were half-a-dozen outlaws with the girl, and Slater was alone. This was one job, they said, where Slater would fail.

McAlister hadn't believed for one moment that Sam Slater would fail. Then, as he began following the bloody trail Sam Slater left behind, he knew that Slater would find the girl. And once he found her, he would have to bring her back to Devil Pass. All McAlister would have to do is wait for him.

McAlister pulled out a piece of jerky and began chewing. He washed it down with a swallow of water, then hobbled his horse and threw down his blankets. He may as well get some sleep. Slater wouldn't be through here before tomorrow.

A HOT, DRY WIND MOVED THROUGH THE canyon, pushing before it a billowing puff of red dust. The cloud of dust lifted high and spread out wide and made it look as if there were blood on the sun.

Three horses came into the canyon. Sam was on one, Cindy on another, and Pardeen's cold, lifeless body was belly-down on the third.

It was mid-morning and they had been riding since first light. Sam was tired, the kind of bone-deep tired that came from long days and short nights and the pressure of having to stay alive. Now, with Pardeen and most of his henchmen dead, there was no need to keep himself on the razor's edge of alertness. Sam could feel the weariness creeping up on him, and as he sat the saddle and let the sun warm his back, his eyelids began to grow heavy and he let his guard down.

The heavy slug whizzed by him, less than an inch in front of his nose. It hit a rock, then let out a banshee whine as it flew away. Sam's hair stood on end and his stomach rose to his throat as he came instantly awake. The deep boom of a distant rifle shot reached his ears.

"McAlister!" Sam shouted.

"What?"

"Come on!" Sam called, slapping his legs against the side of his horse and urging him off the trail. He jerked the reins on Pardeen's horse so that it and Cindy's mount followed him.

There was a second shot and this time the bullet hit one of the spans of a pear cactus. The cactus exploded into little pieces.

"Who's shooting at us?" Cindy cried.

"Get under there!" Sam shouted, pointing to a rock overhang. They rode behind the cover, just as a third shot was fired. Sam swung down from his horse then reached up and pulled Cindy down. He shoved her head down behind a rock and he got down with her.

They were safe here. McAlister would have to come up on them to get a shot, and that would bring him into Sam's range.

"Damn!" McAlister said as he reloaded his rifle. He saw where Sam and the girl ran and he knew he couldn't get a shot at them from here.

McAlister stood up and stretched, then took a few steps back from where he had been sitting, dipped his hand down into the stream, then raised it to his mouth to take a drink. He laughed.

"How much water you got in your canteen, Slater?" he asked under his breath. "How long can you wait?"

McAlister walked back over to his perch on the high rock and waited. Slater and the girl would have to come out some time.

It was late that afternoon when McAlister saw them. At first he wasn't sure it was them, there was only a slight movement way down below. Then, as he looked closely, he saw what was going on.

Both riders were leaning low over the neck of their horses, moving slowly through a twisting ravine, behind an outcropping of rocks and a screen of mesquite. McAlister hadn't noticed that possible escape route when he set up his ambush. They almost made it through, would have, perhaps, had it not been that McAlister caught a flash of red, the girl's dress, out of the corner of his eye.

"Well, now," McAlister said. "Aren't you the clever one? You've found a little ravine that leads out of there, haven't you?"

McAlister looked around quickly, then saw another rock, perhaps a hundred yards away and fifty feet higher. It would make the shot more difficult, but he was sure that from that vantage point, he would be able to see them when they emerged at the far end of the ravine. And if he could see Slater, he could kill him.

McAlister hurried to the new position. He had time, not only because the ravine twisted and turned for quite a ways until it ran out, but also because the two riders were moving very slowly so as not to attract McAlister's attention. As a result, he was in position, lying on his stomach, with the scope to his eye when the two horses emerged.

The moment the two riders came out of the ravine, the horses broke into a gallop.

"Ha!" McAlister said. "Do you think you're clear?"

McAlister aimed at the target, held it in his

scope for a moment, then squeezed the trigger slowly. Even as he was rocked back by the recoil of the exploding cartridge he could see a puff of dust fly away from the back of Slater's shirt. Slater fell from his horse.

The girl's horse continued on for a few feet, then stopped and came back. McAlister opened the breech and slipped in another shell. He thought about killing the girl, too, then decided against it. He wasn't getting paid to kill her. He laughed, then hurried back to his horse, slipped the Whitworth back into the saddle sheath, and started the long ride down to claim his prize.

Nine thousand dollars, he thought. Well, $7,500 as soon as he delivered the body to Devil Pass, then another $1,500 as soon as he managed to get verification of the killing to the proper authorities in Montana.

But it wasn't just the money. No, sir. It was the satisfaction. McAlister was proud of this job. And why shouldn't he be? It was a difficult shot, made under trying conditions. And the man he killed was no easy mark. Besides that, there would no longer be any question as to who was the best in the business. McAlister had just eliminated his closest competitor, and whether the man he shot was number one or number two, it no longer mattered. He was now dead.

As McAlister drew closer, he saw that the red dress was kneeling beside the body. What was the girl doing there? Why hadn't she ridden on while she had the chance? Maybe he should go ahead and kill her. He knew that the man who was paying him for Sam Slater also wanted the girl dead. He was the one who set up the raid on the girl's ranch in the first place. Maybe there would be a bonus for him if he brought in not only Slater's body, but the girl's as well. He had never killed a woman before, but when he stopped to think about it, he didn't suppose it mattered all that much. Killing was killing.

McAlister pulled the shotgun from the other saddle sheath, opened it to check the load, then snapped it shut. As he drew closer still, he urged the horse into a trot and raised the gun.

Suddenly the figure in red stood up and turned around to face McAlister.

"What?" McAlister gasped.

It wasn't the girl! It was Sam Slater, wearing the girl's dress! Almost as soon as he realized that, he saw that Slater had a gun in his hand.

* * *

Sam fired and saw a puff of dust rise from McAlister's shirt. McAlister pitched back out of the saddle as the shotgun flew out of his hand. His foot hung up in the stirrup and his horse bolted, dragging him across the hard, rocky ground for several feet before the foot came undone. Sam hurried over to look down at him. When he got there he saw that McAlister was still alive, though only barely.

"You look awful funny in that dress," McAlister said. His voice was strained.

"Yeah," Sam said. "I wouldn't want to ride into town like this."

"Pretty smart," McAlister admitted. "Who . . . who the hell did I kill?"

"Nobody," Sam said. "That was Pardeen, wearing my clothes and my hat."

"I'll be a son-of-a-bitch."

"I don't understand, McAlister. Why did you come after me? Has the reward gone up that much?"

"Not from Montana," McAlister said. "But someone else offered me $7,500 to kill you."

"Who?"

"Huh-uh," he said. "You don't learn that easy. I will tell you this, though. Me an' you been feedin' at the same trough." McAlister began to laugh. "The same trough," he said. "That's good. That's real good." He laughed again, but the laughing changed to a spasmodic coughing, then he gasped once, and the breathing ended with one, final death rattle.

"Is he dead?"

Sam looked up and saw Cindy standing there. She was wearing only a petticoat and chemise and she kept her arms across her breast, even though she had preserved her modesty, if not her dignity.

"Yeah," Sam said. "He's dead. Now, what do you say we get back into our right clothes?"

As they were changing clothes, Sam thought about what McAlister said about them feeding at the same trough. Then he thought of something else that had been bothering him, though it had been at the very back of his mind until now.

"Cindy. On the morning Pardeen raided your ranch, why was your father there?"

"What do you mean, why was he there?"

"I thought he had to run over to Sweetwater that day."

"No."

"Are you sure?"

"Yes, of course I'm sure," Cindy said. "We were all waiting on the other ranchers to come over and help us put on a new roof that day." She laughed. "Anyway, Pa hated Sweetwater.

He claimed the feed store over there cheated him. He'd go out of his way to avoid the place."

When the little party rode into Devil Pass the next day, they attracted quite a bit of attention. A young boy saw them first and he went running back into town to shout the news. Others came out then and the crowd of citizens formed a parade as they ran along the street alongside the three horses.

"He brought the girl back safe," someone said.

"Who's that belly-down on the horse?" another asked.

"Why, that there's Pardeen."

"He done it! By God, he cleaned 'em all out, single-handed!"

Shorty met them about halfway through town, and though one arm was in a sling and he was getting along on crutches, he hobbled out into the middle of the street to greet Cindy. She slid down from her horse and ran to him. Sam looked back at Shorty and nodded, as if telling him that he had kept his promise, then leaving the two young people embracing in the street behind him, he continued on through town until he reached the Cattleman's Association Building. From the horses and buggies gathered out front, he saw that a meeting was in session. That was good, that was just what he wanted.

Sam pulled Pardeen's body off the pack horse, threw it across his shoulder, then packed it into the building.

"Slater! You're back!" Solinger said. He had been sitting at the head of the table and he stood up as Sam entered the room.

"I've got a package for you," Sam said, dumping Pardeen's body onto the table. Several of the ranchers recoiled in horror.

"That's a rather gruesome package to deliver in here, isn't it?" Solinger scolded. "Couldn't you have just left him on the street?"

"I suppose I could have," Sam said. "But I thought you might want to see him. You know, this means you'll have to get someone else now."

"Yes, I know, your work is all done," Solinger said. "But we won't need anyone else now."

"That's not what I'm talking about. I mean you, Doc Solinger, are going to have to get someone else to do your dirty work, now that your man, Pardeen, is dead."

"My man?"

"Look here, Slater, what the Sam Hill are you talking about?" Baker asked.

"Yeah, that's what I'd like to know."

"What I'm talking about is the fact that Pardeen worked for Doc Solinger," Sam said.

"What?" the others asked.

"How dare you say such a thing?" Solinger blustered. "Why, this is preposterous."

"Is it? Why did you hire McAlister to kill me?"

"What makes you think I did?"

Sam tossed a letter onto the table. "I took this off his body," Sam said. "After he tried to kill me."

"What is that?" Vogel asked, as Baker picked it up.

Baker read the letter, then looked over at Solinger. "It's a letter," he said, "offering $7,500 to McAlister to kill Slater."

"Is that true, Doc?" Masters asked.

"Well, what if it is? Sam Slater is a wanted man. Montana has a reward out for him. I was just supplementing the Montana reward, that's all. There's nothing illegal about that."

"But why would you want to do that? Slater was cleaning out the rustlers for us."

"I didn't make any secret of the fact that I was against all the killing," Solinger said. "I was just trying to stop it the only way I knew how, that's all." He looked at Sam. "Now, if you think you can reason from that, that I was the head of this rustling operation, then I'd like to know how."

"Yeah, Slater, that's a pretty far reach," Baker said. "How do you come up with such a conclusion?"

"I'll leave it up to you to figure out who has gained every time one of the other ranchers is forced out," Sam said. "And I'll leave it up to you to find the missing cows somewhere on Solinger's land. But I do have one question for Solinger. Do you remember the meeting the other morning? The day Hardin's ranch was burned out? Who called the meeting?"

"Doc Solinger," Masters said.

"I'm the president. It's my right to call the meetings," Solinger said.

"Yes, and you told the others that Hardin wouldn't be coming to the meeting because he was going to Sweetwater."

"That's what he told me."

"You're lying. You never told him about the meeting. And the only reason you called one was to make sure none of these men were out at Hardin's ranch when Pardeen and his bunch made their raid."

"You're crazy."

Sam looked over at Baker and Vogel. "Think about it, men. Do you remember what you were supposed to do that morning?"

"The roof!" Vogel said. "We were going to help Hardin put on a new roof."

"Yeah," Baker said. "Why would he go to Sweetwater if . . ."

"Look out! Solinger's pulled a gun!" one of the men shouted.

Sam spun around toward Solinger. He had been expecting this, had hoped for it in fact, and when he saw the gun in Solinger's hand he pulled his own, drawing and firing in the same, fluid motion, doing it so quickly that the noise of his shot covered Solinger's so that they sounded as one, even though Solinger had fired a split-second sooner.

Solinger's bullet whizzed by harmlessly, burying itself in the wall behind Sam. Sam's bullet caught Solinger right between the eyes and the president of the Devil Pass Cattleman's Association fell back in his chair with his arms flopping down upon the arms of the chair and his head lolled back against the back of the chair. Both eyes were open but there was a third opening, a small, black hole, right at the bridge of his nose. Actually, only a small amount of blood trickled from the hole, though the seat cushion was already stained red with the blood that had gushed out from the exit wound.

The ranchers looked at Solinger's body in

shock. It had all happened so fast that, for a moment, they could almost believe that it hadn't happened at all, that Solinger had merely sat back down in his seat. But the drifting cloud of acrid smoke said otherwise.

"Is he dead?" Baker asked.

"As a doornail," someone answered.

Baker looked back toward Sam who had now put his gun away and was looking at Solinger with eyes which were totally devoid of expression.

"Mr. Slater, I reckon we owe you some apologies," Baker said.

"No, Baker," Sam said. "What you owe me is some money."